CRANE HOCKEY

ONE
pucking
LOVE

ELLIE WADE

This book is dedicated to Karrie Oberg—for only she could tell me to drop the other novels I was working on and write a hockey romance immediately because she needed one from me—and I'd listen.

Love you, Karrie. I hope this book makes your hockey romance-loving heart happy!
Thank you for all your love and support.
I'm so grateful for you. xo

PROLOGUE

IRIS

My life was split into two parts: before and after.

Once upon a time, I was young and believed I could conquer the world. Living my best life, I was not only close with my brother but also his best friend, Cade. The three of us were inseparable. Every moment I spent with Cade, I fell more and more in love with him. I didn't realize it in the beginning, when the love was pure and innocent. The emotions I felt were hard to put into words. I just knew that I adored being with Cade. I was happy in his presence. I was fun, confident, and smart—all the things a girl wanted to be. I felt alive. I saw myself reflected back in his eyes, and I saw perfection—the most perfect version of myself. He made me that way. Our connection drove me to grow, pushing myself beyond what I thought I was capable of. It made me fierce, and I craved the power it gave me. I felt loved in a way that I knew only Cade could provide. Even then, I knew what we had was special. He was a treasure, and he was mine. It was never discussed, always just understood that we belonged to one another. I felt that connection deep in my bones, in my soul, and in my heart. My future was Cade Richards.

Or at least, I thought it was. That was before.

One night. One kiss. One rejection. That was all it took to shatter everything. He pulled his lips from mine, and with a look I couldn't quite understand, he shook his head and told me no. It couldn't happen. We couldn't be. Then he walked out of my life. Everything I thought I was, all I thought I knew was gone. He took it with him. He left me alone, a fragment of who I was, questioning where I should go next. Who was I without him? What was my future if not with him? I struggled to understand who I was meant to be. I had to rebuild my self-worth on a pile of broken pieces. Second-guessing everything, I no longer trusted myself. For I was naive enough to be fooled into believing he loved me. Innocence shattered, I vowed to be strong without him. I would excel at everything and succeed in all aspects of my life. Maybe I wasn't all the things I thought I was before, but I'd be them now, at least the ones that mattered. One thing was for sure, I'd never allow Cade to hurt me again.

That was me after a broken heart.

CHAPTER ONE

IRIS

The two-hundred-dollar pen, a graduation gift from my parents, sits perfectly parallel to the large computer monitor atop the shiny mahogany desk. There isn't so much as a fingerprint on the pristine surface. I should know since I scrub every speck of dust and errant smudge with a cotton rag in a daily cleaning ritual prior to leaving the office for the night. Placing my freshly manicured hands on the edges of the keyboard, I shift it slightly, lining it up with the edge of the desk.

My brother teases me that I'm a little OCD, but I'm not—at least not in the clinical sense of the term. I simply want things to look nice. A tidy space doesn't signify an obsession. It means I'm neat and in charge of my work area and my life. And I am.

I've worked hard for everything I have. I didn't rely on my family's money or my father's connections to get me where I am—not when I could help it. My grades and test scores in high school were exceptional enough to warrant my acceptance into the University of Michigan's pre-law program. I can't be certain that my father had nothing to do with me getting into the most prestigious college in Michigan for my undergrad or Harvard law thereafter. The man knows everyone of importance at his alma maters and has made quite the name for himself as one of the state's wealthiest and most successful corporate lawyers. I'm sure he's represented half the board of directors at both universities at some point in his career.

But he had nothing to do with the rigorous schedule that allowed me to earn my undergraduate degree in three years or the top scores I made in law school. I've been nothing if not diligent in my education to get here. I work in one of the best law firms in Michigan, located in Ann Arbor, a mere four miles from the university where I started on this path.

Did I think I'd grow up to be a lawyer like my father? To be honest, no. It was never on the radar until it was. At different points in my childhood, I dreamed of various careers. A dancer, a chef, a decorator, a writer, and an artist were all viable contenders for a time. Yet one very memorable day when I was sixteen changed everything. The night of my brother's graduation party altered the trajectory of my life—who I previously was and what I had wanted escaped me. Suddenly, my old dreams seemed juvenile, my ambitions lacking merit. The events of that day showed me that I had to prove my worth so no one would ever question it again. I was reborn into someone who would be great and accomplish incredible things, and everybody who knew me would see it. I would shine so bright, I'd blind them all.

At twenty-four years old, I'm the youngest lawyer at the Stormberg, Hardy, and Lyons firm. The cases I've been given up to this point have been lackluster, at best, yet I've won them. I'll keep winning until the senior partners see me as the asset I am.

Shaking my head, I quiet the voice that reminds me that the senior partner is my boyfriend, Benjamin Stormberg Junior's, father. Benjamin Stormberg Senior didn't hire me because I'd been seriously dating his son. He brought me on board because he saw my value. Mr. Stormberg isn't the kind of man to do favors, even for his son. He's as tough and unsentimental as they come, further proving that this job is legit.

My father wasn't pleased when I refused to work

for him. He knows I want to make my own way and prove myself. But he doesn't understand how working for my boyfriend's father is different from working for him. I haven't been great at articulating how, but somehow, it is—mainly because it feels different.

I push the chair under my desk and scoop my arm through the straps of my Louis Vuitton bag. I quickly double-check that I have everything I need, and with a final glance toward my desk and a satisfied nod, I start to the office door. Pausing at the large mirror on the wall hanging beside my framed diplomas, I take in my appearance. Admittedly, I tried a little harder with my hair and makeup today. I took the time to curl my long brunette locks into what appears to be effortless waves. My eyeliner is on point, making my large blue eyes seem even bigger. A rosy lip gloss makes my lips appear fuller than usual. I even snuck away for a nail appointment during lunch, which is uncharacteristic of me, as I normally work through my lunches. Yet I wanted today to be perfect. It's Ben's and my one-year anniversary.

This handsome man was a guest lecturer in one of my law classes a little over a year ago. Everything about him mesmerized me. He was sexy and confident. During his lecture, he and I shared some back-and-forth banter, an occupational hazard where lawyers are involved. When class was over and the other students were walking out, he got my attention, calling me up to the front of the hall, where he asked me out. I couldn't believe it. My heart raced as I agreed to go on a date with him. Out of all the women in that lecture hall, he'd asked me. I had stood out to him for whatever reason, which was an incredible feeling.

The rest, as they say, is history.

Today marks a year after the date we agreed to be exclusive. Ben is…well, he's great. He's smart, handsome, and a hell of a lawyer. He's also my first serious relationship. Sure, I've dated, but Ben holds the record as my longest. Not everything has been perfect with Ben, but that's the way of life. Relationships are inherently flawed, and that's okay. It's hard to know for sure, but I think I love him, and tonight, I'm going to tell him just that.

I swipe an errant curl away from my face and head out of my office.

"Ms. Feldmore, I have a few things for you to sign." Nancy, our receptionist, sits behind her desk in the lobby. She holds up a manila folder.

With a smile, I close in on her desk and take the folder from her hands. "Nance, for the hundredth time, call me Iris." I grin.

Nancy is a bubbly blond with the most perfect curls. Think Shirley Temple all grown up. She has one of those faces that is so adorable, you can imagine exactly what she looked like as a toddler. She's my age, and really, besides Ben, my only work friend. The older, grumpy men who work here have no desire to chitchat with me. But that's why I have Nancy, who knows everything about everyone. She takes gossip to a whole new level, and I admit, it's fun.

"You know I have to be professional." She sighs. "Mr. Stormberg gave me an evil stare the last time he heard me call you Iris. I mean, I thought he was going to murder me in the parking garage after work."

"He's a grump but not a murderer." I shake my head, signing the papers in the folder.

She scoffs. "Well, if he wanted to, I'm sure one of his partners would get him off scot-free. That's the thing, never trust anyone who could murder you and get away with it."

I chuckle. "Good words of advice."

"Speaking of grumps, Mr. Lyon's wife called earlier. Their troublemaker son called a fake bomb threat into his high school so he could have a day off."

My mouth falls. "No way."

"Yeah, I know, right? I don't know what will happen, but I'm pretty sure expulsion is on the table," she says under her breath, her eyes wide.

"Well, yeah." I roll my eyes. "You can't do that. Especially with all the real threats going on in schools right now. What an idiot."

"He is. Always has been."

I close the folder and hand it back to her. "What do you want to bet the school ends up with a new library from an anonymous donor, and the troublemaker gets something lame, like a two-day suspension?"

She looks from side to side to make sure we're alone and releases a huff. "Rich people suck...I mean, some do. Not you."

I furrow my brows. "I'm not rich. My parents are, but not me."

She releases a hushed giggle. "That's totally something a rich person would say."

"Stop it." I chuckle.

"So what's the plan for the big anniversary night?" She changes the subject.

"I don't really know. Ben's been so busy all day that I haven't been able to see him. I'm going to check with him now. I'm sure he has something planned."

"Of course." She nods. "Well, I can't wait to hear all about it tomorrow." She quirks a brow.

"You know it," I say before giving Nancy a wave and heading across the lobby to Ben's office door.

I knock softly before I turn the handle and step in.

Ben is on the phone. He gives me a curt nod and holds up his finger to indicate he'll be a minute. I close the office door and walk over to his shelf, where a dozen framed photos with pictures of Ben and important people stand on display. It's very cliché, and it doesn't escape my notice that no photos of us are displayed after a year of dating. To be fair, I don't have a framed picture of Ben in my office, either. Then again, I don't have photos of anyone.

Ben paces back and forth behind his desk, his tone angry. "Don't worry, Curt. We're going to get them." He pauses. "Absolutely. We're on it. Great. Talk soon." He swipes his thumb across the screen of his cell and tosses it onto his desk. He looks toward the ceiling and rolls his head from side to side while releasing a sigh.

"Everything okay?" I ask hesitantly. The tense air in the room is making me very uncomfortable.

He blows out a breath and holds me with his stare. "Same shit. Different day. Right?"

I take a step toward him. "So you're okay?"

He rolls his eyes. "Of course I'm okay, Iris. Dealing with idiots is part of our job. Is it annoying? Yes. Do I let it affect me? No."

I press my lips in a line, not entirely believing his statement. I'm not sure what he feels qualifies as "affecting him," but I'd say he's definitely affected. He's radiating pure rage.

"Okay." I nod, trying to figure out how to bring up our anniversary plans.

As I said to Nancy, I'm not sure what they are, but I'm certain we have them.

"So tonight..." I hedge.

He shuffles through some papers on his desk. "I'm working late tonight."

I can't help the hurt that surfaces in my voice. "It's our anniversary."

"What?" Ben hurls the question toward me. It's so abrasive I can almost feel the single word punch my gut. He furrows his brows before shaking his head. He lets out another breath and pins me with a stare, this one more gentle than before. "I mean, yes... of course I know it's our anniversary, Iris. I'm sorry. I just have a lot on my mind and wasn't thinking clearly." He takes a step toward me and grabs my hands in his. "Can I take a rain check on your plans?"

My plans?

"Of course." I force a smile. "You're busy. It's fine."

"You sure? I know you probably had something really special planned for us tonight, but it's not a good time for me. Things here need my attention."

"Absolutely." My heart hammers in my chest. I force down the emotion threatening to spill over.

He releases my hands and leans in to kiss me on the cheek. "We'll celebrate this weekend, yeah?"

"Sure."

"Thanks, babe. I knew you'd understand." He presses his lips to mine for a second before returning to his desk.

He sits in his big leather office chair and starts clicking the mouse while he stares at the computer screen. He hasn't said as much, but I'm clearly dismissed.

Adjusting my purse in the crook of my arm, I stand tall and walk toward the door.

Before I step out of the office, Ben calls, "Iris?

I turn to look over my shoulder. "Yeah?"

"You look beautiful today."

A genuine smile finds my face. He noticed that I put extra time into my appearance for our anniversary. Things like this make me think I might love him.

CHAPTER TWO

IRIS

With my heels clicking across the concrete of the parking structure, I hurry to my car. Sliding into the seat, I close the door, lean back against the headrest, and release an audible sigh. Tears threaten to surface, but I keep them at bay. This is what being in a relationship with a sought-after lawyer is like. It's not personal. I know Ben would much rather be out with me than stuck in his office all night. It's just part of the job.

My phone buzzes in my purse. I pull it out to find a text from my brother.

Beckett: Hey, Sis! Just wanted to remind you that bye week is coming up. My invitation stands.

I shake my head with a scoff, the corners of my lips turning up into a smile.

I already told you I can't take off a week to go hang out in Barbados. I have a job.

Take the time off. I'm sure you've earned it.

My brother, Beckett, is two years older than me and one of the starting forwards for Michigan's NHL team, the Cranes. I rarely get to see him because of his rigorous schedule. If he's not traveling for games, he's practicing. Growing up, we were always really close, even on the days I wanted to kill him. He's the most infuriating person I know, yet he's impossible not to love. He has charm coming out of his ass. Lately, life has kept us apart, and I have to admit, I miss him. A relationship through text isn't the same as an in-person one.

The mid-season bye week is coming up, and Beckett and his teammates live for this week off. They always rent some extravagant mansion in an exotic location and party for a week straight. Though I've never been to one, these weeklong parties are things of legend.

I can't. Sorry.

Yes, you can. And bring that hot slutty secretary of yours.

Nancy is not a slut!

You're the one who told me she was! LOL

Oh, well. She's really nice.

You act like I think being a slut is bad 😉

True. Spoken like the true slut you are.

Exactly. There's no shame in my game.

> You're an idiot. Don't you have a game to play?

We're in LA, remember? Won't be on until 10 p.m. your time.

> Oh, that's right.

You're watching the game? Yes?

> Always do.

That statement is a flat-out lie. I rarely do, but my reasons have nothing to do with Beckett. He'd be crushed if he knew the truth. After every game, I search the internet for his highlights so I can congratulate him and sound like I watched him in action.

Think about Barbados. I miss you.

> I miss you, too, but the answer is no. Don't worry, you'll be busy with all your puck bunnies. You won't even notice I'm not there.

I'll always make time for you.

> Good luck tonight. Play hard. Don't get hurt. Love you.

> Love you too.

> And stay out of the penalty box!

> No promises.

I set my phone into the cup holder, feeling so much lighter than I did moments ago. What seemed so heavy doesn't feel that way anymore. It really doesn't matter if we delay our anniversary celebration until this weekend. I'm not sure why I let it affect me so much.

Starting my car, I pull out of the parking structure. It's a cold, dreary day—typical of Michigan in January. The sun has already set as is normal for this time of year. It's dark when I get to work and dark when I leave. That alone could be a cause for my sudden onset of moodiness. After twenty-four years of living in what seems like months without sunshine every winter, one would think I'd be used to it. But I don't think I'll ever be used to it.

The back of my car slides across the slick pavement as I turn onto the road, and I tighten my grasp on the steering wheel. I love my Audi RS, but it is not a great winter car, which is painfully obvious every time I drive it when there's even a slight dusting of snow on the roads.

As I drive, thinking about Ben and this past year, I realize I don't need an extravagant evening to celebrate my relationship with him. I pull into the Whole Foods parking lot. If he can't make it out, I'll bring our anniversary dinner to him. If an office picnic doesn't say romance, then what does? I know he told me he was busy, but the man has to eat.

I'm filled with a renewed sense of excitement as I enter the store. Something about picnics is so sexy. Maybe I've been conditioned over the years while reading books and watching films about love that featured picnics, but I think they are insanely romantic. I find everything I need in the store, including an adorable basket, blanket, wineglasses, a bottle of Ben's favorite wine, and some candles. The prepared food bar is stocked with dips, cheeses, and foods sure to be delicious. When I check out, I have more food than Ben and I could possibly eat, but the spread will be amazing.

Loading the items into my trunk, I think this may be the type of anniversary dinner we were meant to have. Our lives will always be busy. That's a given. It's going to be about fitting our celebrations in around our schedules.

The firm's parking spots are vacant, save for Ben's car and a couple of others. I'm relieved that most people have gone home for the night. An empty office will just add to the ambiance of the romantic picnic.

Opening the trunk, I arrange the items in the basket before sliding my arm through the handles and lugging the heavy thing out.

With excited steps, I walk through the halls of the office, passing one empty room after the next. Pride swells in my chest just thinking about Ben working away on his cases when all the partners have gone home. He'll surpass all his superiors in no time. I have no doubt he'll be partner someday in the not-too-distant future.

I reach his office at the end of the hallway. With a large smile on my face, I pull down on the handle, and the door swings open.

Nancy, in all her nakedness, leans over the grand mahogany desk while Ben pulls her blond curls and pounds into her from behind. Their naked bodies are covered in sweat, indicating that they must've been engaged in this activity for a while. With his free hand, he grips her hip, pulling her forcefully against him.

My smile falls, as does the picnic basket I'm holding. I barely hear the crash of the items hitting the floor. I'm frozen by the view in front of me. I know exactly what I'm seeing, yet my brain can't make sense of it. None of it seems real.

The two of them turn their faces toward me, and their eyes widen in shock. Nancy opens her mouth, I think to say something, but she quickly clamps it closed. Ben releases his hold on Nancy's hair, presses his hands against her ass and slides out of her.

"Iris, let me explain," he says, bending toward the floor to retrieve his slacks.

I hold out my hand and shake my head before taking a step back. Ben calls after me, but I don't process his words. Blood rushes through my brain, and it feels as if I'm underwater. Everything is muted. Hurrying toward my office, I step in and look around the cold interior. I snatch the pen that my dad gave me from the desk and my framed diplomas from the wall.

I give the space a final scan. Certain there's nothing else here I need, I step back into the hallway and close the office door.

There's not a lot I'm sure of at the moment. Yet as I race—as fast as my heels will allow—back out to my car, I know without a doubt that I won't be returning to my office.

I'm done here.

CHAPTER THREE

CADE

The music pounds through the speakers as the bodies jump around the bar in a mix of dance and celebration. We're coming off five huge wins in a row against fierce competitors and are feeling good. Going into our bye week, we're on pace to break some records this season. A lot can happen during the second half of the season, but this group of guys is undoubtedly the best team that Cranes hockey has had in years.

Most players on any NHL team are talented. They wouldn't be on a professional hockey team if they weren't. But it takes more than talent to make a winning team. It takes the perfect balance of skill, personalities, and teamwork. Something about this group of guys on this team, at this time, feels—as corny as it sounds—like magic. We just work.

"Heartbreaker!" my best friend and fellow wingman on the team, Beckett, calls as he all but stumbles toward me, a hot, barely dressed woman on each arm.

Beckett Feldmore has been my best friend since we were ten years old. There is nothing I wouldn't do for this guy, and vice versa. He's referred to as "Feltmore" by the team and proudly wears the badge of team slut with pride. The guy has no shame. Yet in his defense, he's more beautiful than Miss America, so he doesn't have to work too hard to whore around. Girls flock toward him.

On the opposite end of the spectrum, the team calls me Heartbreaker because I don't sleep around and instead leave broken-hearted girls wherever I go. I feel that's a little dramatic. But once a nickname sticks, there's no getting rid of it.

I pull the Dum Dums sucker from my mouth. "What is it, Beck?"

"I wanted to introduce you to Stacey!" He guides a leggy brunette toward me.

She shoots Beckett a glare. "It's Macey."

"Close enough." He shrugs.

"Hey, Macey. Nice to meet you." I extend my free hand to shake hers.

She puckers her lips in an oddly unnatural way and drags her manicured fingernail down my arm. "Beckett said you might want to go back to the hotel suite with us later," she purrs.

"Did he?" I quirk a brow and look over Macey to find Beckett wearing a shit-eating grin. "Yeah, unfortunately, I can't make it."

She crosses her arms. "Really?"

I shrug. "Yeah, plans…you know?"

Beckett places some money into Macey's friend's hand and tells them to go get everyone another round of drinks at the bar. The women grin and take off.

"Would you stop trying to set me up?" I grumble and stick my sucker back in my mouth.

"Dude. Why?" He holds up two hands, palms out. "You've played hard to get long enough. It's time."

I roll my eyes. "I just don't do random hookups. It's not my thing."

"But that's just it, man. You don't really have a 'thing.'" He lifts his fingers in air quotes. "Besides, not hooking up and being a sugar fiend, which, by the way, half of the world thinks you're a fentanyl pop addict because you always have a fucking sucker in your mouth."

I chuckle. "They do not. First of all, half the world doesn't watch hockey. Second, those who watch don't see me sucking on suckers. They see me playing. I may be in an occasional social media post with a sucker in my mouth, but I highly doubt everyone thinks I have a drug problem."

"Really? Then why are you always chosen for the 'random'"—there he goes with the finger quotes again—"drug tests?"

I throw my head back in laughter because it's true. Every time we're supposedly randomly chosen for a drug screening, I'm on the list.

"Let them test me." I shrug. "I have nothing to hide. They're plain ole Dum Dums suckers, man."

"I know that, but all I'm saying is it wouldn't hurt you to step out of your comfort zone now and again, shake things up," he says.

"By whoring around?" I lift a brow.

He laughs. "It's a fun option."

"Anyway, what time are we leaving for your parents' house tomorrow?"

Beckett groans. "Leave it to Iris to plan a stupid-ass anniversary party during bye week. Their anniversary isn't even until next month."

"Well, I'm pretty sure she planned it during our bye week so you could go. You wouldn't be able to make it in February."

"Yes, I know," he snaps. "But that's going to push back Barbados by a whole day. It's just annoying is all."

"It will be good for you to go home. You rarely do."

He glares. "Stop trying to be all logical and just let me wallow in my pity party, okay? Yes, it will be nice to see my parents and Iris, but you know I live for bye week. How is Barbados going to beat out Fiji from last year if I'm not even there for the day?"

"If anyone can make it happen, it's you."

Beckett doesn't return my grin.

Penelope Stellars, our team's PR rep, closes in on us with a look of disgust on her face. She's wearing her usual form-fitting pencil skirt and top, and her deep red hair is pulled up in a tight twist. I don't know if I've ever seen the woman smile. I'm not exactly sure what her job is supposed to be, but she ends up working really damn hard to control the narrative on social media to make our team look good. The owners want to keep all the crap we pull and drama we cause out of social media. She makes us all look like stand-up guys, which isn't an easy feat. It's no wonder she's always pissed off.

"Cade Richards!" she calls my name in a huff.

"What is it, Penny?"

"Dreven is about to beat the crap out of some kid at the bar." She holds her fisted hands in front of her face and presses her mouth against them. She shakes her head and continues. "Some kid, looks to be a smart-mouthed eighteen-year-old, said that Halko's form is superior to Dreven's."

Beckett scoffs. "Halko? The weak-ass goalie from Vancouver? No way. He's like a limp noodle out there. Dreven is a hundred times the goalie Halko is."

Penelope whips her head to Beckett. "I couldn't care less about the facts of this ridiculous pissing contest. All I care about is the fact that if that hothead touches that kid, it's a lawsuit waiting to happen." She turns her stare back to me. "And since you're the only player in here who's not wasted off his ass, maybe you can help me get him out of here before he does something that will cause me a lot of strife?"

Our goalie, Gunner Dreven, is one of the best in the league, but it's true—he has a very short fuse. The last thing the team needs going into bye week is an assault charge.

"Absolutely," I say to her. "Come on."

Beckett follows Penny and me to the bar where Gunner stands arguing with a guy who, like Penny said, can't be a day over eighteen.

I step between the two. "Are you old enough to be in here?" I ask the kid.

"Yeah," he huffs out with a glare of his eyes.

"Isn't this a twenty-one-and-up bar?"

The kid furrows his brows and puffs out his chest. "You know what? You sucked tonight, too. You should've totally made that shot in the third period.

Feldmore gave you the perfect pass, and you messed it up."

"Hey, Rick!" I shout to one of the bar's bouncers. "This kid needs to go. He must've snuck in. He's only seventeen."

Rick comes over and takes the guy's arm. "Let's go, kid."

"I am not seventeen!" the guy shrieks, but it doesn't escape my attention that he doesn't say he's twenty-one because I guarantee you he's not. As Rick leads him toward the door, the kid calls over his shoulder, "You're an asshole, Richards! Try laying off the Fenty, and maybe you'll play better!"

"God, that kid's a dick, and what is Fenty?" I ask the guys.

"He's talking about the fentanyl lollipops." Beckett laughs.

"What the hell?" I scoff.

"I told you, man." Beckett grabs my shoulder.

"You do have quite the obsession with candy," Penny states.

I groan. "There is nothing wrong with liking suckers. They have less than twenty-six calories a piece with no fat. They're a hell of a lot healthier than half the shit you all are consuming in here tonight. It's a habit, okay? And not a bad one."

The truth is, Margaret, my last foster parent and the closest person I've had to a mom, always had a bowl of them in the foyer. Margaret was the only foster placement that wanted to keep me, despite being way too old to raise a teen boy, and I'll always be grateful to her for that. At ten years old, I'd been to more foster homes than I could count. I always thought I'd eventually just age out of the system. Then Margaret took me in and loved me. She gave me a chance at a childhood. I met Beckett and Iris, and for the first time in my life, I felt like I had a home.

My Dum Dums obsession started back then. The sucker symbolized something for me, something that made me feel good and loved. I feel like I've had one in my mouth since. So yeah, it's a habit, but not one that's hurting me or anyone else.

Changing the subject, I turn to face Dreven. "Why the hell you going to fight a kid, man?"

He pins me with an annoyed stare. "I wasn't going to fight him. But I wasn't going to let him disrespect me, either."

"And how were you going to stop him? By using your words?" Penny argues. "I doubt it. Can you just please keep your shit together? Tomorrow, you leave for Barbados, and after months of dealing with your shit, I can finally have a week of peace!"

"What? You're not coming to Barbados with us?

What if we need help staying in line down there?" Beckett asks.

Penny's chest rises as she pulls in a slow breath through her nose. "Bye week is my week off, and believe me... I need it. I need one freaking week away from you lunatics, or I'll seriously go insane. I don't know why grown men can't keep their shit together. Just give me a week, okay?"

"Hey." Beckett rubs her arms, wearing a look of compassion. "We'll keep our shit together just for you. I promise."

She rolls her eyes and all but stomps off.

"I don't think she likes us." Beckett watches her leave.

"I don't think she likes you," I say to Beckett. "Or you," I say to Dreven. "I don't cause her any problems."

Dreven raises his hand, signaling the bartender for another. "Being boring isn't a flex, Heartbreaker."

Beckett hits his hand on the bar top, laughing. "Right? I've been trying to tell him that."

"You all are a bunch of assholes." I shake my head, plopping another sucker in my mouth.

CHAPTER FOUR

CADE

"All the pics of the place look great. Uh, the infinity pool... What I wouldn't give to be in there right now." Beckett stands outside his car as he scrolls through the pictures being posted in our team's group message thread. "And look at this hottie." He turns the cell toward me.

I look across the top of the car to Beckett's cell. "I'm sure there's more than one attractive bikini-clad woman in Barbados."

"I wouldn't know." Beckett clicks his phone off and slides it into his back pocket.

I shake my head, closing the car door, and walk around the back. "You are quite the baby today."

He rolls his eyes. "I'm just tired. You know I hate

the time zone shit."

Partying until the early morning hours in Seattle last night and then traveling back to Michigan today caused us to lose several hours of sleep with the time difference. Most of the guys pound an espresso and get on with it, as is evident by the ones already having a great time in Barbados. Yet Beckett needs his beauty sleep, or he's a grouch to be around.

"Suck it up, and put on your happy face," I warn.

He nods. "I will, of course. I'm not going to ruin my parents' party or anything. I'd just rather be napping."

The Feldmores' grand house sits atop a hill. The corners of my mouth tilt up in a smile as I take it in. I love this place. Growing up, I thought it was a mansion, though Beckett always said it was just a house. It's definitely not *just a house.* Despite its massive size, everything about it screams wealth. I'd venture to say the upkeep on the landscaping alone costs a small fortune. Before I met Beckett, I'd only seen a house this beautiful on TV shows.

Mansion or not, this home holds so many happy memories for me. It's good to be back.

A flower-covered table sits at the beginning of the pathway leading up the stone walkway. Atop the table are stands holding real floral leis. The sweet smell of the flowers is a welcome sensation on this otherwise dreary January day.

Beckett chuckles. "Iris." He shakes his head. "She can't spare a day to come hang out in Barbados, but she can plan an extravagant themed party. I thought she didn't have any time. My sister has always loved a good theme." He takes hold of a lei and places it over his head.

I reach for a white one made of orchids and do the same. "Your parents had their honeymoon on Maui, right?"

He dips his chin. "They sure did."

We follow the tiki-torch-lit path up to the house. As we step into the foyer, we feel transported to a fancy party in Hawaii despite the chilly winter temps outside. A ukulele sounds through the house as the late Israel Kamakawiwo'ole's, better known as IZ, version of *Somewhere Over the Rainbow* plays. Iris has always loved this song. The house smells of hibiscus, and tall vases of tropical flowers are placed along the walls. Candles adorn the tops of every surface, illuminating the house's interior with a soft glow.

"Boys!" Mrs. Feldmore calls out as she hurries toward us, a wide smile on her face. She's wearing a long flowy dress in a colorful floral print. "You made it!" She hugs Beckett, kissing his cheek before repeating the greeting with me.

"Of course we made it, Mom," Beckett says.

"Wouldn't miss it for the world," I offer.

She shakes her head. "I know how busy you are, and I'm so happy you're here. Come on." She takes Beckett's hand. "Let's go find your father. He'll be thrilled to see you."

Thrilled isn't a word I'd ever use to describe Mr. Feldmore. The man rarely smiles and has always been reserved and stern in nature. He's not mean or unlikable, per se. He's just not the kind of father who tossed a ball with Beckett or hugged either of his children. He's very much the provider, while Mrs. Feldmore is the nurturer. What her husband lacks in affection, she gives out tenfold.

She grabs my hand with her free one and squeezes. Her hands clasped with ours, she leads us through the house, stopping to say hi to guests and make sure everyone knows that her boys are home.

"Yes!" She smiles from ear to ear in response to a guest's comment about how well we've been playing this season. "They're fresh in from Seattle after another win. Can you believe it?"

We weave our way through a crowd of people. "Mom, today is not about us," Beckett states.

"Oh, nonsense. I'm going to brag about my boys as much as I want. I'm proud of you. I've watched the two of you play hockey together since you were ten years old. You've worked so hard to get where you are, and I'm going to shout it from the rooftops."

She looks from side to side. "Now, where is your father?"

"Probably in the study smoking a cigar," Beckett offers.

She nods. "Oh, I bet you're right. Come on." She tugs us forward.

As Beckett predicted, we find Mr. Feldmore in his office with a stogie between his fingers.

"Honey, look who's home!" She leads us into the smoky room.

Mr. Feldmore stands from his leather chair. "Beckett." He holds out his free hand and shakes his son's before shaking mine as well. "Cade."

"Father," Beckett greets his dad with a nod. "Happy anniversary."

"Happy anniversary, Mr. Feldmore," I say.

"Thank you. Glad you could swing by. Your sister has gone overboard, as usual," he states before placing his cigar between his lips. "Not that she has anything better to do, I suppose." He blows out a long plume of smoke.

Mrs. Feldmore shakes her head. "This was a very kind thing for her to do for us. I'm very grateful for all the work she's put in. It makes me feel like we're back in Maui."

"What did that comment mean? That she has nothing better to do?" Beckett takes a step back so he's out of the way of the cloud of smoke hovering in front of his father.

Mr. Feldmore huffs. "Well, since she up and quit her job, she has a lot more free time than she used to."

"She quit her job?" The question falls from my lips.

Mrs. Feldmore presses her lips in a line. "Yeah, almost two weeks ago, now. We don't know why. She hasn't wanted to talk about it."

"She didn't tell me she quit. Where is Iris anyway?" Beckett questions.

"Last time I saw her, she was heading out to the pool house," Mrs. Feldmore offers.

Beckett turns to leave. "I'm going to go find her."

"Wait, Son. I had a few things I needed to talk to you about." Mr. Feldmore places his cigar in an oversized ceramic ashtray and steps around to the back of his desk. When he's in that position, it's never a sign of happy conversations to come.

He doesn't mention my name, so I take that as my cue to leave. With a smile and a nod, I back out of that stuffy office as quickly as I can. The air beyond the office feels lighter and definitely smells better. I've never been a fan of smoke. Too many of my earlier memories—and not good ones—are associated with the scent. Not that any of my foster placements smoked expensive cigars, more like Marlboro reds or menthols, but to me, smoke is smoke.

I pass the spread of food, which looks like it was transported from a luau in Hawaii. The platter of kalua pork smells especially delicious, and I make a mental note to come back for some of that as soon as possible. The rumble in my stomach reminds me that all I've consumed today is coffee, but eating will have to wait.

Opening the tall door to the backyard, I spot Iris immediately. She's distracted, her petite frame is shadowed by the large white box she's holding as she makes her way across the path from the pool house to the main house. I steal a second to take her in, and my chest hurts. She's so beautiful. She always has been, but now, even more so. Her brown hair with golden highlights cascades over her bare shoulders in carefree waves. She's wearing a long flowy floral dress as well. But whereas Mrs. Feldmore's says "sophisticated mom," Iris's says "Hawaiian beauty queen." Her eyes are drawn downward as she navigates over the stone walkway, but I only have to look into my mind to see their brilliant hue. Her large bright-blue eyes have come to me in my dreams more than I'd admit aloud. I've always been fascinated by them.

My heart twists. I've missed her. God, it's been so long. Sure, she comes to games here and there, but I get little more than a few minutes of pleasantries during those encounters.

I have this overwhelming desire to talk to her for

hours like we used to. Since graduation, I've seen her on the major holidays, her high school and college graduation, and any other noteworthy occasions that Beckett has decided to visit home. Yet I can't remember the last time I've had a real conversation with her.

Except that's a lie.

I remember our last deep conversation like it was yesterday even though it was eight years ago. *Has it really been eight years since our graduation?*

The past eight years of my life have been a blur. Beckett and I played for the University of Michigan's hockey program and both got drafted to the Cranes. There's been little time for anything else other than hockey. I worked my whole life to get to where I am. Failing wasn't an option.

I've been living my life, and Iris hers. She went to undergrad and then Harvard Law. We've both been chasing our dreams, leaving little time for what we were in the past. The truth is, she was my best friend, along with Beckett. The two of them were my everything and still are. Things are just different now.

A piercing scream pulls me from my thoughts as the sight of Iris tumbling forward flashes before me. The white box goes flying into the air as Iris puts her hands out, softening the blow as she hits the ground.

I run forward. "Iris!" Sprinting, I reach her in a matter of seconds. "Iris, are you okay?"

She scoots up onto her knees, her hands splayed out in front of her as she looks up at me. Her lips tremble as her brilliant blues fill with unshed tears.

A wave of deja vu hits me hard, causing me to breathe in cold air.

"You live here?" I ask Beckett as I stare at the giant house before us, my mouth falling open in awe. "It's a mansion."

Beckett laughs. "Dude, it's just a house."

If Beckett only knew some of the places I've lived, he wouldn't say that, but I don't expect him to understand. He doesn't mean to be insensitive; he just doesn't know. He's lived here his whole life with his parents and sister. It's not his fault that he's grown up with everything. Just as it's not my fault that I've grown up with nothing. Or at least, that's what I tell myself.

Maybe things are really going to change this time. Margaret promises that she's going to keep me. She says I'll never have to worry about where I'm going to live again because I'll always have a home with her, and I want to believe her. None of my other foster placements ever said that, so maybe she's telling the truth.

Things do feel different this time. I made a friend, a real one. I don't know what Beckett sees in me, but for some reason, he thinks I'm cool.

"My dad had a rink built in the back for me. I'll show

you the basics today. I have extra sticks and gear that you can have. It's fun. You're going to love it." Beckett invited me over to play hockey. It's really all he wants to talk about, and since I've never played, he insists on teaching me. "In the winter, it's the best, though, because the rink ices up, and that's when the real fun starts."

A little girl steps out the front door. Her ponytail swings from side to side as she walks toward us, carrying a tray of beverages between her hands.

"That's Iris," Beckett says. "Father's trying to teach her about the value of money. He's going to build her an art studio if she earns some money to put toward it. Though he said the same thing to me about my rink. I didn't earn any money, but he had it built anyway. I told Iris that, but she's determined. She's always been a suck-up."

The little girl comes closer, focused on the tray of cups she's carrying.

"No one's gonna buy a cup of warm lemonade," Beckett yells.

Iris looks up, startled. Her eyes go wide as she trips, and the tray of cups flies out in front of her as she tumbles to the ground.

I run past Beckett until I reach his sister and kneel before her. She looks up at me with the biggest blue eyes I've ever seen. Her lips tremble as streams of tears roll down her cheeks. "It's okay. I'll help you fix it. Come on." I extend my hand to her.

Hesitantly, she looks from my face to my hand. Finally, she places her small hand in mine.

I kneel beside her. "Iris, here." I extend my hand to her.

She doesn't take it. Instead, she sits back on her legs and presses her palms against her thighs. "Is it ruined?" She nods toward the box.

I stand and take a step toward the box. Carefully, I open the lid. I'm not sure what the cake looked like initially, but I'm positive it wasn't this. There's a jumble of color and cake all over the box. Picking up the box, I tilt it toward Iris so she can see the contents.

She stares motionless at the mess of frosting. After a second, she brings her palms to her face and starts crying, full-on back-heaving sobs. I lower the box to the ground and hurry back to her.

"Hey," I say gently. "I'll fix it. I'll go out and get another one." Kneeling, I wrap my arms around her as she cries. "It's going to be okay." I kiss the top of her head.

Her tears don't abate for quite some time. I'm not sure what to do, so I just hold her and wait. Eventually, she leans into me, wrapping her arms around my back. She leans her face against my chest as more tears come.

"Rosie, hey. Look at me." Her old nickname gets

her attention, and she tilts her tear-soaked face toward me. "What's going on?"

She chokes in a few breaths. "Everything is falling apart. Everything." She chokes on the last word. "I don't know what to do anymore. I just... don't know."

Her words are hauntingly sad. I haven't a clue what's going on with her right now, and that thought sends a wave of shame through me. But it's clear she needs a friend, and I'm going to be the best one I can be.

"First things first, the cake. What did it look like? I'll go get another one."

She shakes her head and leans her cheek against my chest. "You can't. I had it delivered from the bakery that made their wedding cake. They're located in New York City." She sniffs. "It was perfect. A white cake with coconut cream filling and buttercream frosting. It was covered in beautiful pink and white lilies made of frosting. My mom's wedding bouquet was made of lilies." She sighs. "I just give up. I give up, Dummy."

The last sentence makes me smile. She hasn't used her childhood nickname for me in so long. I stand and pull her up with me. "Speaking of dummies..." I grab a Dum Dums sucker from my pocket. "For you, while I'm gone."

She takes the sucker from me and shakes her head.

"I know you think these things are magical, but they're really not, Cade."

"Look at the flavor." I quirk a brow.

A small grin finds her mouth and releases a puff of breath. "Coconut."

"Exactly. Now, I won't be able to get to New York and back with a special order cake, but I'll see what I can do. Okay?" I rub her bare arms, suddenly aware of just how cold it is out here.

"It's fine. Just forget about it." She shrugs. "They just won't have a cake. I was bound to mess something up."

I extend a hand again, and this time, she takes it. I pull her up from the ground. "I don't think so. I'm getting you a cake. You can't throw the perfect Maui-themed anniversary party and not have a cake, right?"

"You think the party's perfect?" she asks softly.

"Yeah," I huff. "I do. Then again, everything you do is."

She rolls her eyes. "Well, that's not true."

Retrieving the cake box, I pick it up and hand it to her. "Here, take this back to the pool house. Don't throw it out. I guarantee you it's still delicious, and your mom will want to have some later. Freshen up, take a few deep breaths, and when you're ready, rejoin the party. Maybe save Beckett from your father."

An almost smile plays on her lips. "Oh, gosh. Does

he have him trapped in his office?"

I nod. "Yeah."

She furrows her brow. "You said freshen up. Do I look awful?"

"No, never. Impossible."

"I look like a raccoon, don't I?" She pouts her lips.

I look at her face. The black from her mascara circles her eyes and trails down her cheeks in streaks. "You look beautiful, Iris. You always do," I say honestly before leaning down and kissing her forehead. "Just make a stop at the pool house bathroom mirror before heading back, okay? I'll be back soon with a delicious Hawaiian-themed cake in no time."

As I hurry toward the house, I pull another sucker out of my pocket. After unwrapping it, I pop it in my mouth and smile when the taste of coconut hits my tongue. What are the odds? I turn back toward the pool house to find Iris standing in the same place, watching me.

Grabbing the sucker stick between my finger and my thumb, I raise it in the air. "Make sure to try yours," I call out. "It'll make you feel better."

"I doubt it," she shouts back, but she pulls off the wrapper and sticks it in her mouth anyway.

"Magic!" I smile.

She shakes her head with a grin, and it hits me just how much I've missed that smile.

CHAPTER FIVE

IRIS

My laughter echoes off the stone-tiled walls as I take in my appearance. "Beautiful, my ass, Cade." I chuckle. I officially have more mascara on my face than on my lashes. In fact, I don't think there is any left on my lashes at all. "Well, at least he gave me a heads-up," I say to myself. I could be walking into a room full of people looking like this. I suppose it could always be worse.

Wetting some tissue, I attempt to clean up my face, but it's no use. There's no salvaging the makeup look I spent thirty minutes perfecting this morning. I squirt some hand soap into my palm and start lathering it over my face. It dawns on me that I'm using antibacterial hand soap on my face, something my skin hasn't experienced since my mother introduced me to high-end skincare at the age of ten. *Oh, how the mighty have fallen.*

I suppose if I am to look at my life with a glass-half-full mindset, now that I'm as low as I can possibly go, I can only go up from here. Right?

That's what Cade does for me—makes me see the positives. He's always been this encouraging influence and comfort in my life. When I'm strung so tight I can hardly breathe, he swoops in and loosens the stress strangling me. It seems so effortless for him, too. He knows exactly what to do and what to say to help me breathe a little easier.

God, I've missed him.

It's no secret that our friendship hasn't been the same since he went off to college. We both got busy living our lives and reaching for our individual dreams. He had Beckett and hockey. I had college, the law firm, and… Ben.

Ugh.

I shake my head to clear the thought. Nope. Not going there. Think positive.

Grabbing the hand towel, I dry my face.

I take in my fresh-faced appearance in the mirror. Well, it's not the Hawaiian princess look I had going earlier, but it's better than the zombie raccoon look from moments ago.

With a final glance, I drop the towel and exit the pool house. I have to go save Beckett.

Inside the main house, I open the thick wooden door to my father's office, and a mix of cedar, wood, leather, and spices hit me as I step through the wall of smoke. I find my brother exactly where I knew he'd be.

"Beck!" I hurry toward him.

His shoulders fall in relief as he releases a breath, and a huge smile forms on his face. "Sis!" He stands from one of the deep brown leather chairs that face my father and hurries toward me. Pulling me into a hug, he buries his face in my hair, whispering, "Thank you! Don't leave me."

Pulling back from the embrace, I address my father. "I need Beckett's help." My words are firm. I've learned to always act more confident than I feel when dealing with my father. He can sense weakness from a mile away.

"Well, alright." He frowns. "We'll get back to this conversation later, Son."

Beckett nods and follows me out of the office.

"What was he talking to you about?" I ask when we've left my father and his smoke-filled office behind.

"Fuck if I know." Beckett scoffs. "I think he was blabbing on about money, investments, retirement… shit like that. He's worried I'm not spending my money wisely. Why can't he just be a normal dad?"

I grin and raise a brow. "Well, are you spending your money wisely?"

"Hell no! I'm living in the moment, baby!" He gives me a wink and his famous Beckett Feldmore grin. My brother's smile has gotten him almost anything he's wanted his entire life. He's so handsome and charming that it's hard not to be dazzled in his presence. The only person who doesn't fall for this charisma is my father.

He pulls me into a hug, lifts me off the ground, and spins me around. "God, I've missed you."

"I've missed you, too." I hug him tight. "Have you eaten?" I ask as he sets me down.

"No, and I'm starving."

"Come on." I lead him toward the kitchen. "You know, it wouldn't hurt to put some of your money away or invest it. An injury could take you out of the game tomorrow. It's not a bad idea to plan for your future."

"Nope!" he shouts. "Mini-Dad is not going to lecture me today. This is a party!" He moves his body in some weird dance moves as he closes in on the food spread.

"Don't call me that." I give him a faux glare. "I'm not like Dad."

He picks up a plate and spoons a pile of kalua pork onto it. Grabbing some sweet Hawaiian rolls, he says,

"Maybe not. Now that you've quit the firm." He tosses a piece of pineapple into his mouth. "I need to hear all about that, by the way," he says through a mouthful of fruit. "Working with your man wasn't all it was cut out to be?"

"He's not my man anymore."

"Oh shit… the plot thickens. I'm sorry, Sis. I have a feeling there's a whole story behind that one?"

"Yeah. One that is better told over a bottle of vodka and not a plate of pork."

He gives me a knowing look. "Got it. I'll take a rain check on that story until tonight. But I have to say, I never did like Benny-boy. He always gave me douche vibes if I'm being honest."

"Well, you're not wrong."

Mom walks in, holding a Mai Tai in each hand. "There are my loves! My babies! Home together. You know this doesn't happen enough, and it needs to happen more!" she all but shouts, her eyes more squinty than usual.

"Mom, how many Mai Tais have you had?" I crack a smile.

She shrugs and releases a happy sigh. "I couldn't tell you. Here, you have this one." She shoves one of the fancy glasses into my hand. "I'm just having the best time. This is such a wonderful party, sweetie. Thank you so much."

"You don't have to thank me, Mom. I'm happy you're happy. Maybe go get Dad from his office and make him join the fun." I readjust the pink paper umbrella in my glass.

Mom purses her lips. "Why is that man always work, work, work? He really needs to learn to cut loose a little."

"That he does," Beckett agrees.

Mom looks around the space as if suddenly aware. "Where's Cade?"

Beckett follows suit. "Oh yeah... where is he?"

"He ran out to get something for me. He'll be back soon."

"Okay, great! Well, I'm going to go get your father, and Iris honey... I really liked the look you had going earlier, but you're right. You're beautiful just the way you are. You've never needed makeup." With that, she scurries past us.

"Thanks, Mom," I grumble under my breath.

"What is she talking about?" Beckett asks, oblivious.

I shake my head. "Nothing. Come on."

We find a quiet corner of the house, taking a seat in one of the few comfortable sofas in the place. "So tell me everything. I feel like I never see you," I say.

"Because you don't." Beckett chuckles. "But now that you're boyfriend-free, job-free, and responsibility-free… that is about to change. You have no excuse. You're coming to Barbados."

My head falls back against the sofa cushion. "No, Beck. It's not my thing."

"I knew it!" He grins. "It was never about all that other stuff. You just didn't want to come."

My lip curves to the side. "Well, yeah…"

He laughs. "You're ridiculous. Come on. You can relax. You can party. You can sit by the pool and read the whole time. Whatever you want to do. You can make it your thing. Plus, we'll get to hang out."

"You get one week during the whole nine-month season to do whatever you want, and you want to chill with your sister?" I pin him with a stare.

"Of course… among other things. But definitely the sister part, too. Come on. It's been years since we've had a proper hang-out—you, me, Cade."

Cade…

"I don't know." I sigh.

"Seriously, Iris! I'll do anything. I'll throw some of my money in a 405C thing."

I laugh. "You mean a 403B?"

"Whatever. Any of the numbers and letters. I'll do it. I mean, I have more than I can spend sitting in the bank anyway. If you want to invest it for me, it's all yours. Just come. Please."

He's right. There's no excuse for me not to go. I'm

letting an insecurity from eight years ago hold me back, and why? I'm twenty-four years old and no longer the brokenhearted sixteen-year-old. Where has my fear led me? To a job, partner, and life that is no good for me, one that doesn't bring me any joy? I need to seriously re-evaluate my priorities, and poolside in Barbados isn't an awful place to do it. At the very least, it can't make things worse.

"Fine."

Beckett's eyes go wide. "Fine, as in you'll come?"

I roll my eyes. "I'll come."

"Whoo!" Beckett screams, pumping his fist in the air. He's so silly I can't help but laugh. "We're going to have so much fun, Sis. Seriously. I have no idea what happened with Ben and your job, but I know you well enough to see that you need a break. This will be good for you."

"Yeah, yeah. Eat your food and tell me about your life. We'll get into my crap later."

He shovels a heaping forkful of the pork into his mouth. "What do you want to know? It's all a blur if I'm being honest."

"What about last night? I'm assuming you all partied after the win?"

He sticks the tip of his thumb in his mouth, licking the sauce from it, and a smile forms. "Oh yeah. Last night was lit."

CHAPTER SIX

IRIS

"You hate it?" Cade asks.

He brought back a hundred cupcakes. I have no idea where he found this many cupcakes on a Sunday night on such short notice, let alone how he had a perfect lily frosted on top of each one, but I'm stunned and deeply grateful.

"Oh my gosh, no. They're perfect." Emotion is thick in my throat. "She'll love them."

"They're vanilla, not coconut, but I thought the lilies turned out well." He tilts his head to the side, admiring the cupcakes.

"Are you kidding? It looks like a big, beautiful bouquet. I love them. Thank you so much." I wrap my arms around Cade's middle and look up at him.

It's been a while since we've been this close. I take in his features, and my heart beats wildly in my chest. He's matured in his looks. He still wears his short brown hair all spiky and disheveled. His beautiful hazel eyes, full lips, and dimple above the right side of his mouth are the same. Yet his face has filled out some over the years, his jaw more defined, making his overall appearance more manly, grown-up. It's been eight years since my face was this close to his, and I guess anyone will grow up in that amount of time. There's a slight curve to his nose that wasn't there before, evidence of the two times he broke his nose since high school. Cade Richards isn't one to back down from a fight on the ice, despite his gentle nature off it. And yet—even that new imperfection only adds to his perfection.

"I'm glad you approve." He leans in and kisses me on the forehead.

I jerk my body away from his. "Yeah, definitely!" I blurt out. "Come on. Let's go show Mom."

We find my parents mingling among their guests, and of course my mother loves the cupcakes. Tears fill her eyes when she sees that each one is decorated with its own lily. My chest fills with love, and I'm pleased she's so happy. She would've bawled at the re-creation of the wedding cake I originally had for her, but I'll take her happy tears over the cupcakes. Thanks to

Cade, she still gets a meaningful dessert to end her thirtieth-anniversary party.

The party winds down, and the guests say their goodbyes. One by one, the lei-wearing crew disperses until they've all left.

As I close the front door behind the final guest, I let out a relieved sigh.

Planning elaborate parties is something I truly enjoy. But I can't deny the relief I feel when they're over.

"Honey, this was perfect. It's one of the best parties I've ever had. Thank you so much." My mother pulls me into a tight hug.

"You're welcome, Mom. I loved doing it."

She releases me, and my dad reaches out and grabs my hand in his, giving it a squeeze. "Thank you, Iris," he states, and I hold in the tears, overwhelmed by his gesture.

"Of course, Dad." That's all I manage to get out.

The two head toward the second floor and their master bedroom, and I hold my palm, still warm from my father's touch, against my chest.

It's done. The party is over. I've spent every waking moment for the past week and a half planning this night. The second I walked away from the law firm of Stormberg, Hardy, and Lyons with nothing but a pen and two framed diplomas, I've thought of nothing but this party.

My heart races as my feet carry me to the kitchen. The large granite island top is covered with food. Half-eaten entrées and fruit platters are scattered over the surface. The visual cue that the party is officially over hits me in a visceral way, and I internally start to panic. The climb to this night kept my mind occupied, but the inevitable fall weighs on me now. It's so heavy, it's paralyzing.

After this, I have nothing. No job, boyfriend, or idea what to do next.

I open and close my hands. They feel swollen as the blood rushes through them. Inhaling deeply, I struggle to breathe. Air reaches my lungs, but there's no oxygen.

I can't breathe.

Placing my palms against the bar, I lean forward. My chest rises and falls in an attempt to allow air access to my suffocating lungs. My chest aches as my body trembles. Panic fills me as the room spins. I can no longer feel my limbs, and as soon as that thought resonates, my legs give way.

Squeezing my eyes closed, I wait for the impact of my body hitting the floor. Instead, strong arms wrap around me and pull me up.

"Shh... just breathe, my Rosie girl." Cade pulls me

against his chest and rubs his hand up and down my spine. "Deep breath in and out. You're okay."

I allow Cade to hold me while I focus on my breathing. Slowly, I come back to myself. The enormity of my failings is again at the forefront of my mind, and the tears start falling.

No words are spoken. Cade's strong arms secure me against his body as the tears roll down my cheeks. He continues to run his hand up and down my back in a soothing gesture of comfort. It's not lost on me how weak I must look at this moment, but I can't find the energy to care. I'm too broken to be embarrassed.

I'm neck-deep in an existential crisis at the ripe ole age of twenty-four. Everything I've worked for, thought I wanted, or believed I had is just... gone. The sad thing is I'm not even sure if I truly wanted any of it to begin with. The mere thought of putting away all this uneaten food has cracked open an abyss of sadness within, none of which I can even make sense of. At this moment, I don't know who I am. I'm too lost to be found.

Cade kisses the top of my head. "Do you trust me?"

I nod.

Of course I trust him. He's been one of the guiding lights in my life, even if he shouldn't have been. Despite his actions being the catalyst for my entire failure of a life, I still trust him. I always will. It's a sad day knowing that Cade Richards could beat me down a hundred times, and I'd still get up for that one hundred and first time.

Though, even as I think that thought, I know it's not true. Cade broke my heart eight years ago, and I'm still fighting the effects of that loss. I would never survive it a hundred times over. The truth is, I couldn't survive it again. Even one more time would be too devastating to come back from.

"Okay, wait here," he says before hurrying from the room.

A minute later, he stands in front of me with a blanket, two forks, and two bottles of wine. He drapes the blanket around my shoulders and takes my hand in his, leading the way from the kitchen.

"Where's Beck?" I ask, wiping my tear-soaked face with the corner of the blanket.

Cade stops before we reach the back door and points toward a sofa across the room. Beckett lays across the leather, a plush blanket draped over him, no doubt put there by Cade. His mouth is open, and his hand hangs off the couch as he sleeps. "He needed his beauty sleep."

Despite how very shitty I feel, I chuckle. It's probably for the best. My brother is a royal grump when he's tired.

Cade leads me out the back door and across the

walkway where I fell earlier until we're inside the pool house.

The lights beneath the water's surface emit a soft blue glow, illuminating the whole room.

Cade releases my hand from his and pulls two lounge chairs together at the end of the pool. No longer needing the blanket around my shoulders in this warm space, I toss it onto a table and take a seat in one of the chairs. Cade opens the bottles of wine and hands me one.

"Riesling. My favorite," I say before taking a sip of the sweet white wine.

He places the box of cake I dropped earlier beside me and sits down with his own bottle of wine. Opening the box, he hands me a fork.

Hesitant, I stare at the pile of cake and frosting. Cade picks up a piece with his fork and holds it toward my mouth.

"For you," he says.

Opening my mouth, I take a bite. A groan escapes.

"Good?" He chuckles.

"So good." I nod.

He gets a forkful of cake for himself and tries it. "Agreed. So much better than the cupcakes."

I shake my head. "The cupcakes were delicious."

"But not like this."

"Where did you get them anyway?" After scooping

up another bite of cake, I wash it down with a swig of wine and immediately feel better than I did moments ago.

He brings his bottle of wine up to his lips and takes a sip. "You know the bakery owned by the Obergs?"

I nod.

"Well, I've known them forever, attended Sunday school with their boys. They were close to Margaret. I've hooked them up with front-row seats to our games many times. I knew they'd help. Gave 'em a call and told them the situation. Mrs. Oberg opened the store and added lilies to an order of cupcakes she made for a birthday party tomorrow."

"What about the order of cupcakes for the party?" I ask.

He shrugs. "Said she could whip up another batch and that it wasn't a problem."

I take another bite of cake. "That's so nice. I'll have to send them something to thank them." I stare at the water in the pool. With the lights shining from beneath the surface, it looks like water from the Caribbean, a bright tealish blue. The sight is calming. "How is Margaret?"

"Um... the same." Cade's voice lowers slightly. The tone would be unrecognizable to most, but I hear the shift in his voice, the sadness. "I'm going to visit her tomorrow before I fly out."

"I'd like to come," I offer. "It's been way too long since I've visited."

"Sure. If you're not busy."

I scoff. "I'm not busy."

He turns to me, squinting his hazel eyes, and chews on the corner of his bottom lip. "I get the feeling that's a loaded statement. Tell me everything."

Tell me everything.

It's what Beckett, Cade, and I have always said to each other when we want all the tea spilled. It means no nonsense, no beating around the bush, no vague answers—just the facts and all of them.

I turn away from Cade and face the pool again, a frown finding my face. I have no desire to talk about everything. It all hurts too much. If I'm being honest, a big part of everything involves Cade, and I have too much pride to share that part.

Being here with Cade is bittersweet. I'm not sure how to feel about it. Despite the hurt it brings, I can't deny that I've missed it and crave it.

CHAPTER SEVEN

CADE

I can see her weighing the options. Does she talk or not? There's no question she has a lot to say. It's up in the air whether she'll share. Yeah, back in the day, "tell me everything" meant just that. But somewhere along the way, everything got fucked up. She's different now. Hell, I've changed, too. We all have. What we had in high school isn't what we have now. While that hurts, it's normal. We've grown up.

As much as it pains me to admit, I know nothing about certain aspects of Iris's life. Maybe that's my fault? Who are we kidding? I'm definitely to blame. I felt us growing apart, and I didn't stop it. I backed off when I shouldn't have.

She stares into the pool, her big blue eyes glassed over as she takes another swig of wine.

"Maybe it will be easier to do a question-and-answer format? Give me five questions, and *everything* beyond that will be left for another time. How does that sound?"

She turns to face me, lying on her side. "Fine. But I control full veto rights."

"Of course. You don't have to answer anything you don't want to." I hold her stare. Fresh-faced, without an ounce of makeup, she's, without a doubt, the most beautiful woman I've ever seen. "Tomorrow's Monday. Why aren't you busy?"

"Because I don't have a job," she answers.

"Why don't you have a job?"

"Because I quit."

"Why did you quit?"

"Because I walked in on Ben screwing the secretary on our anniversary."

"Oh, Iris. I'm so sorry. That's awful."

She raises a brow. "That was three. You have two more."

I nod. "Right. Okay, um… are you okay?"

"Clearly not, but I'll get there."

"What are you going to do next?"

She shrugs her shoulders. "I have no idea."

I take in her features, the worry lines on her brow,

the way she's gnawing at her lip, and the hurt and pain in her eyes. So much more is going on here than a cheating boyfriend. I'm just not sure what. "One more question?" I raise my brows.

"Fine." Her answer is a sigh, but I'll take it.

"So you have the cheating ex-boyfriend and no job situation, but I feel like there's more to it than that. What's really going on, Iris?"

She bolts upright. "Veto," she protests and stands from the lounge chair. She brings her bottle of wine to her lips, tilts her head back, and chugs the remainder. "I'm going inside."

"Wait." I hurry to my feet. "Not yet." I'm not entirely sure why I'm protesting. I'm so exhausted I could fall asleep standing up. I have to get up early tomorrow to visit Margaret before getting on a plane to Barbados. Despite all that, I don't want this night to end. More accurately, I don't want her to go.

"Cade." She blows out a breath. "It's been a long day. I'm tired."

"I'm tired too, but it's not time to call it a night just yet."

She puckers her lips, suppressing a grin. "And why is that?" She lifts a brow.

I extend a hand toward the water. "We haven't swum yet."

She drops her head back in a laugh, the sound

echoing off the walls. Her laughter does something to me. It makes me feel unsettled in the best way. It's addicting. "I'm not going swimming," she states.

Tilting my own wine bottle back, I down the contents before removing my shirt. "Come on," I urge as I unbuckle my pants and slip them off until I'm standing in just my boxer briefs. Without hesitation, I dive into the warm water.

"Cade!" Iris chuckles when I emerge from beneath the water. "What in the hell are you doing?"

"What does it look like?" I smirk. "Swimming. Now get your butt in here. You can't leave me in here all alone."

She crosses her arms over her chest. "I never agreed to this."

"Please?"

"Ugh," she groans. "You're so annoying, Dummy." The way that nickname twists my heart is unreal. She's the only person to ever use it, and before tonight, she hasn't said it in so long.

She unzips the back of her flowy dress, and it falls to the tiled floor, leaving her standing before me in a matching set of lacy undergarments. My breath hitches, and I splash my hands against the water to cover the sound. Seeing her perfect body makes me feel scandalous, and I know I should turn away. But I can't. She's stunning, and though I've seen her in a bikini hundreds of times, something about her tonight leaves me utterly breathless.

"You going to jump in, or what?" I call out, breaking the tension.

She rolls her eyes with a shake of her head and dives in.

There's a smile on her face when she emerges from beneath the water. "It's so warm."

"It is." I look past the foggy floor-to-ceiling windows that line the pool house to the wintery weather beyond.

Iris swims past me. "I always thought it was weird how my dad kept it heated all winter when neither of my parents come out here to swim, but I have to admit, I'm glad he does."

Stretching my arms above my head, I push off the side of the pool and swim across. The movement feels good on my tired muscles.

We spend a few minutes lazily swimming back and forth across the pool until we both end up in the middle, floating on our backs. The full moon is visible through the giant skylight above us.

Iris breaks the silence. "Are you sure you want me to come with you tomorrow to visit Margaret? I don't have to go. I mean, if you want time alone with her, it's fine."

"No, she'd love to see you. I think she would, at

least. I'm completely serious when I say you're more than welcome to come. It will be nice to have a friend there." A *friend*—the word tastes sour when it falls from my lips. I haven't been a very good friend as of late.

"So Beck isn't going with you?"

"No. He's catching the first flight out. Doesn't want to miss a second more of his party week."

Iris chuckles. "He's so ridiculous."

"Agreed."

The conversation tapers off, and we continue to float in silence and take in the beautiful moon.

I lose track of time. Long minutes pass until Iris releases a sigh and says in a soft voice, "I'm going to Barbados."

I stand and face her. "You are?"

She follows my lead. No longer in a back float, she faces me. "Yeah, Beckett begged me, and I figured, why not? I have nothing better to do."

I grin. "That's good. It'll be fun." I can't deny that spending an entire week with Iris appeals to me.

"Maybe." She shrugs.

"No, it will. It will be good for you to get away, relax, clear your head…figure stuff out. You know?"

Reaching her hand out, she moves it through the water, causing ripples. She raises her face, and her eyes pierce my heart. "Yeah, I guess."

Her beautiful blues hold my stare, and so much pain and worry reside in their depths. It kills me that I don't know what's going on with her. "Come here." I grab her hand and pull her toward me. Her eyes widen in shock, but she doesn't stop me. I see the moment she decides to trust me. The decision flashes across her face right before I pull her against my chest and wrap my arms around her.

I hug her tight. "I'm so sorry."

She tenses, her arms straight at her side. After a few seconds, she relaxes and returns my hug, circling her arms around my waist. "Why?"

I hold her and rub my hand up and down her back. "I've been an awful friend, Iris. I should've touched base with you more often. Beckett and I graduated and took off… and it wasn't cool. It was shitty, really. You deserved better. There's so much I should've said and didn't. And now… you're clearly going through something I know nothing about, and it's evident how crappy of a friend I've been."

"It's fine," she states.

"But it's not."

She takes a step back, pulling out of my embrace. Her eyes are wet with unshed tears. "People grow up and leave. It's normal."

"I'm always here for you, Iris. I'd never leave you," I reassure her.

She scoffs, and a frown finds her face. "But you did."

Her words are a dagger to my heart, and I'm left speechless.

She backs away and moves through the water until she's climbing up the ladder and out of the pool. She grabs a towel from the oversized basket beside the pool and wraps it around her body.

"Your room is all set up for you." She moves toward the exit and says over her shoulder, "I'll see you in the morning."

With that, she steps out into the cold, leaving me alone in the pool, speechless. There's a deep ache in my chest and a chill in my veins. Goose bumps cover my skin, and suddenly, the water doesn't feel so warm.

CHAPTER EIGHT

CADE

The building was designed to be welcoming with its fountain, birdbaths, and elaborate landscaping. However, the fountain has been shut off for months, the birdbaths are frozen, and the flowers dead, making the place appear how it feels—dreadful.

I hate coming here. It's the most prestigious facility I could find, voted best in Michigan on care, staffing, and amenities. But it's not Margaret's home, and no amount of bingo games or smiling staff members will make it so.

"Ready?" Iris startles me, and I have to refrain from flinching.

I wring my hands against the steering wheel. For a second, I forgot I wasn't alone. The whole drive here I was lost in thought, this visit weighing heavily on my mind. Iris and I didn't really speak much, partly because of the lingering awkwardness of last night but mostly because of exhaustion. I'm coming off two nights of very little sleep, and the way Iris has been sipping her enormous mug of coffee like it's her lifeline, I know she's tired too.

Pulling in a breath, I open the car door. "Yeah, let's go."

My heart beats rapidly as I step into the building and sign in at the front desk. I had called ahead to let the staff know we'd be stopping in this morning. I know part of the program is following a strict schedule to give the patients a reliable structure and reduce outbursts. I wanted to make sure I visited during an ideal time. The residents have free downtime for the next hour, so the timing is as good as it gets.

"Follow me, Mr. Richards." The little blond nursing assistant smiles and starts down the hall. "Your mom is going to be so happy to see you," she lies. It's not a malicious act. Sometimes I just don't think people know what to say.

I give her a noncommittal grunt.

She looks over her shoulder. "I'm serious. She's always in a better mood after your visits. We've all noticed it."

"Well, if that's the case, then I'm glad," I say, hoping her words ring true.

She stops in front of Margaret's room and knocks twice before opening the door. "Margaret," she sing-songs. "You have guests."

"I have guests?" I hear the closest person I've ever had to a mother exclaim, and I have to swallow the lump in my throat.

"Have a good visit," the nursing assistant says quietly. With a smile and a nod, she exits the room, leaving Iris and me.

I take a step farther into the space and see that not much has changed since the last visit. The rooms are set up and furnished like apartments. It doesn't feel like a hospital room.

"Hi, Margaret." I smile.

She looks up from the magazine in her lap and grins.

I met this woman sixteen years ago, and I swear she looks exactly the same today as she did then. Small frame, thin, white hair that she wears atop her head in a tiny bun. Her face is covered in wrinkles from a life-time of smiles and laughter.

"Can I help you?" she asks, her voice pleasant.

"Well." I pull a picture from my wallet and hand it to her. "I was told you might know what kind of dog this is?"

She takes the photo from my hand, and her smile grows. "You bet I do! This is only the best breed of dog there is. It's called a dachshund, which means badger dog in German. You see, they were originally bred in the seventeenth century to climb into badger holes and pull them out. The hunters used and traded the badger's pelts, you see. Why, were you thinking about getting one?"

I take a seat on the sofa across from the recliner Margaret's in. Iris sits beside me.

"I'm not really sure. What do you think?" I ask.

She nods. "Oh, I think that would be great. Those little guys are fun, playful, and very clever. They're really a hoot." She chuckles. "They're also fiercely loyal and will adore you. I'd suggest starting with one, though, since you're new to the breed. They can get very jealous if you give your attention to any dog but them."

"Really?"

"Oh yeah...I used to breed dachshunds, you know? I have stories for days."

Iris leans forward. "Are there any stories that come to mind that you wouldn't mind sharing?"

"Of course. Let me think." Margaret scrunches her face in thought.

Turning to Iris, I give her a weak grin. She must know how hard it is for me to see Margaret and not have her remember who I am. I appreciate her being here with me as these visits have become more difficult for me over the past few years.

Margaret started losing her memory, at least noticeably, the year I started college. It was little things at first, but the severity of her memory loss declined rapidly. It was difficult being away at college, too. The time apart made it that more obvious how quickly her mind deteriorated. We researched facilities together, and I insisted on putting her in the best one we could find. She liked this place because it felt like a community of retirees more so than a medical nursing home. At first, we couldn't afford it as her insurance only covered the bare minimum. But the second I signed with the Cranes, I transferred her here. That was four years ago when I was twenty-two.

It's been two years since she's remembered me. Two years of visiting her as a stranger. I've learned over my visits that the only topic of conversation that always works is her love of dogs, specifically dachshunds since she bred and raised them her entire adult life.

Margaret's eyes go wide with a memory, and her mouth turns up. "I just thought of one. So my son, Cade…"

I suck in a breath, and my body freezes. It's been at least a year since she has mentioned me by name. Margaret fostered many children in her youth.

According to her, most of their placements were temporary. Kids came and went, sometimes reunited with a biological parent or an extended family member. I was her last foster placement, and she's never referred to me as one of her kids, like the others. I've always been her son. She always told me that I was her last because she knew I was destined to be hers, and she wanted to focus her energy on raising me. I thought that was just fluff to make me feel good and assumed she stopped after me because she was getting older and couldn't handle more children. Now that she doesn't remember most things, I suppose I'll never truly know.

She continues. "He used to call every dog we had 'hot dog' because he said they all looked like sausages with legs. He was so funny. I swear he did it just to make me laugh. Well, Cade went through a hot dog stage, like the food. I swear there was a whole year when he only ate those processed things." She grimaces, making me chuckle. She's always hated hot dogs. "One night, I grilled a bunch of hot dogs for dinner and placed them on a plate on the table. I went outside to retrieve the veggie kabobs still on the grill. When I came back inside, my four dachshunds were standing on top of the kitchen table and the plate of hot dogs was empty. They'd eaten every last one!" She laughs.

"What happened next?" I asked, already knowing the answer.

She throws her hands up. "Those four little rascals threw up hot dogs all night."

Iris and I laugh.

"But, you know...my Cade...he cleaned up every last pile of puke. He's such a good boy." She looks fondly at a framed picture of her and me from when I was twelve. We found that pictures of me from adulthood confused and even upset her. All her memories of me are from when I was young.

"He sounds like a wonderful son. You're so lucky to have him," Iris says.

Margaret nods. "Oh, I am. I love my boy, and he loves his momma." She looks at the door. "I'm sure he'll visit soon."

"I'm sure he will." Iris smiles reassuringly.

Another piece of my heart breaks as Margaret stares at the closed door to her room. She shakes her head and hands me back the picture of the dog. "Well, is there anything else I can help you two with? I think my morning swim class is in a few minutes, and I'd hate to miss it. I must keep in tip-top shape, you know?"

"Of course." I stand from the sofa. "Thank you for letting us visit."

I've found the second she suggests another activity,

I need to go. She's had some intense outbursts when I've overstayed my welcome.

"Anytime. If you decide on that dog breed, let me know. I'd love to hear how it's going."

She won't remember this conversation tomorrow, but I nod in agreement. "Do you mind if I give you a hug?"

She opens her arms wide. "Of course, I'm a hugger!"

Bending down, I wrap my arms around her and squeeze her. It's not long enough, but it's as long as a "stranger's" hug should last. "Thanks again."

I stand and head toward the door while Iris hugs Margaret and says her goodbyes.

"You got a handsome one there," my mom says. "He's got a good soul, too. I can tell these things. Hold on to him, honey."

"Thank you, Miss Richards. It was great to meet you."

"You too, darling."

Iris follows me out of the room, and I close the door behind us. We're silent as we walk back to the car. Once seated inside the vehicle, Iris turns to me, her eyes wet with tears. "I'm so sorry, Cade. I had no idea she was that bad."

"It's okay." I shrug, starting the car and turning up the heat. "Today was actually a really good day. Sometimes she can't remember who she is, let alone stories from her past. That's the first time she's mentioned me in over a year, so it was nice. Heartbreaking but nice."

"I knew she had dementia and was in a home, but I guess I never thought that she wouldn't remember you or me. I'm not sure what I thought that visit would be like, but..."

"You didn't expect that?" I finish for her.

"No." She shakes her head. "Not at all. It's so sad, and I'm so sorry. I should've checked in with you. You shouldn't have to go through all this alone."

"It's okay, really. It's not on you. I suppose we both have dropped the ball on this whole friendship thing. We'll do better, okay?"

She nods.

"Plus, I wasn't completely alone. I have your brother."

She huffs and buckles her seat belt. "Yeah, Mr. Empathetic Listener of the Year."

I chuckle. "He's not that bad of a listener. He tries."

"Well, from here on out, we'll start being better friends to one another. Deal?"

"Deal. First stop on our friendship reunion. Barbados. And after that, you're coming to some of our games now that you have no excuse not to." I shoot her a wink.

"I suppose." She sighs.

The sound brings a smile to my face, and overall, I'm relieved. In terms of visits, that went as well as it could. Now, I have a week in Barbados with my teammates and Iris. A foreign sensation—*hope*—fills my chest, and I have to admit, I like it.

CHAPTER NINE

IRIS

Cade is literally inches away from me, and I miss him. God, how I've missed him. My heart has ached for him for so long. The fluffy white clouds below us and endless blue skies out the window of my first-class seat do little to pull my attention from the man beside me.

I steal a glance to my left to find Cade leaning back against the headrest, AirPods in his ears, and a sucker in his mouth. His eyes are closed, but he's not sleeping. My stare zeros in on the dimple on his right cheek, the little divot making the horny butterflies in my stomach dance erratically.

Ugh. No. I can't let my mind go there.

There is no *there* with us. But maybe after all these

years, we could go back to a real friendship. Beckett has always claimed him as his best friend, but he was mine, too. I was just as close to Cade as my brother was. The only difference between the friendships was two years and an insane crush, which led to a failed kiss that ruined everything. If I was a boy, Cade and I would still be friends. Or maybe if he was a hideous, ogre-looking man. Yet even as I think it, I know it's not true. It may seem cliché, but I was in love with Cade's soul, which was only amplified by the pretty package it came in.

Obviously, I'm still attracted to him. But his gorgeous exterior isn't what causes the constant ache within. It's everything else. I miss the way we would talk for hours. Not only did he listen to every word I would say but he'd *hear* me. You can get almost anyone to listen to you, but hearing is on a whole different level that only happens with people who truly care. Cade understood me in a way that no one else did. As close as I am with my brother, even he doesn't get me the way Cade does.

I miss the way my nickname Rosie rolls off his tongue. The nickname stemmed from a little eleven-year-old Cade bringing me a "flower like my name" one day, only for me to inform him that he'd brought me a rose and not an iris. Something so simple created a term of endearment that only he uses, one that would make everything okay with a single utterance.

I miss how he made me laugh and could turn any bad day around. Life with Cade was joyous. To others, he's more reserved. He's not loud and outgoing like my brother. Everyone loves Beck because he gives himself to everyone. Cade is different. He only shares his real self with those he loves. I think it stems from years of foster care. Cade doesn't trust easily. To the important people in his life, he's the sun—warm, perfect, and free. Something is sacred about being one of the few who Cade loves and trusts. Getting parts of a person as wonderful as Cade that no one else has access to is special. I miss being one of his people because, the truth is, it made me feel special, too.

A touch of my hand causes me to jump in my seat. I jerk my head to the side.

"I didn't mean to startle you." Cade grins and nods toward the beverage cart in the aisle. "Do you want anything?"

"Um, just a water, please."

Cade hands me a bottle of water and takes a chug of his own bottle. "Everything alright?"

"Yeah, I was just thinking, and I zoned out."

"Anything you want to talk about?" He quirks a brow. "I'm a great listener."

I chuckle under my breath. "Yeah, you are but no,

nothing important. I've never been to one of these bye week parties. How crazy is it going to be?"

He smirks. "What are you imagining?"

"Oh, I don't know, a weeklong orgy, naked women everywhere, maybe some tigers walking around," I tease.

"That's what you imagine? And you still came?" He laughs.

I roll my eyes. "Well, I don't know. Hockey players are whores, right? This is your one down week all season. I just figured it would get a little crazy."

"Not all hockey players are whores."

"Beckett talks like they are."

Cade shakes his head with a smile. "Well, yeah... your brother is a whore, but that doesn't mean everyone else is."

"So what are we talking, then?"

"There will be girls, yeah. But if there is sex, it's done in the guy's room. Sorry to disappoint. We've never had a giant orgy." He chuckles.

"I'm not disappointed," I protest.

"Okay." He scrunches his lips and raises his eyebrows. "Sure... anyway, definitely no tigers, though Gallagher posted in the group chat that a monkey stole his plate of pasta off one of the tables out back last night. We'll have to wait until we get there to decide whether we believe that. You know Gallagher can be a bit of a whiner. And last, I can't promise that one of the guys won't emerge from their room naked and drunk off their ass at some point, but generally, everyone wears clothes."

"So what do you all do normally?"

"We drink, hang out in the pool, watch movies, play cards... relax. We're constantly working, so in truth, we just want to have a week of downtime before heading into the next couple of months of training and games." He sips on his water before screwing on the cap. "But if you have your heart set on that orgy, I can talk to the guys and see what I can do."

I hit his arm playfully. "You know I don't."

"Okaaay." He reaches into his pocket, pulls out a sucker, and tips it in my direction.

"No thanks."

He shrugs and pulls the paper off the sucker before plopping it in his mouth.

"You're so weird." I grin.

"I'm not the one dreaming of orgies and rogue tigers."

"Stop." I nudge him again. "Don't be spreading that rumor."

"I would never. It's our little secret, Rosie."

There he goes, melting my heart.

Friends. I can do this.

The colonial-style estate the guys rented for the week is stunning. Perched along the pristine coastline of the island of Barbados, it's nestled amid lush tropical gardens and swaying palm trees. A grand entrance, including a sweeping driveway lined with vibrant bougainvillea flowers, greets us as our driver pulls up to the place. The mansion's facade boasts a crisp white exterior adorned with ornate balconies, intricate wrought-iron details, and large arched windows.

I step out of the car as Cade thanks the driver. He grabs our bags from the trunk and smiles my way. "What do you think?"

"It's gorgeous." The warm Caribbean breeze and bright sun heat my skin.

"Alright, let's get inside and see if we can't find you that orgy."

I slap his arm. "Stop. I'm serious. Not another word." I follow him up the stone walkway to the entry door. "You know Beckett wouldn't ever shut up about it."

"I told you, it's our secret."

Stepping through the front doors, we're greeted by a lavish foyer, adorned with marble floors, glittering chandeliers, and exquisite art pieces that evoke a sense of opulence. Music can be heard in the distance.

"I think this'll do," Cade states.

"Yeah, I'd say so." My head tilts back, taking it all in. "It's quiet."

"They're probably out by the pool. Come on."

I follow Cade through the spacious living area with its plush sofas, intricately carved wooden furniture, and floor-to-ceiling windows. A grand staircase leads to the second story of the place.

Cade sets our bags at the foot of the stairs. "Until we figure out which rooms are ours." We continue through the house until the massive pool comes into view beyond the wall of windows. "Well, there are some of them."

Beckett is sprawled out on a teal pool float in the shape of a seashell with his eyes closed. A handful of other players lounge around the pool area, some beneath the shade of the palm trees and others on the deck. Several women I haven't seen before are scattered among them. Pop music plays from the speakers attached to the exterior walls.

"Feltmore!" Cade barks, startling Beckett so much that he tips off his pool float and into the water.

He emerges with a laugh. "Jeez, Heartbreaker... a quieter entrance wouldn't be awful, you know. It's about time you all got here."

"What are you talking about?" Cade grins. "You've been here...what, two hours?"

"Yeah." Beckett grunts. "And look around. Total lame fest."

"Where is everyone else?" I ask.

"Sis." Beckett smiles as if he's just realizing I'm here. "You came."

"I told you I would."

"I know, but I can never be too sure with you. Anyway, everyone is sleeping. Apparently, they had quite the rager last night. Some of them were just heading to bed when I arrived this morning. And..." He shoots me a mock glare. "We missed it."

"Get over it." I scoff. "You'll have plenty of time to party."

"Which rooms are ours?" Cade asks.

Beckett walks through the pool and up the steps until he stands on the tiled patio. "About that. There's only one left."

"What?" Cade and I belt out in unison.

"How is that possible? This place is massive," Cade states.

Beckett throws his hands up in mock surrender. "Hey, don't shoot the messenger. You know how we always tell the team to bring people but no one really ever does? Well, this time, everyone did. There are double the people we thought there'd be. Honestly, the only reason there's even one room left is because I bribed Calloway and Dreven to share a room this morning when they were wasted. Otherwise, you wouldn't even have one."

"It's fine," Cade says. "I'll just stay with you. Iris can have the room."

Beckett shakes his head. "No can do. I'm already sharing."

"With who?" I cross my arms.

"Vicky."

"Who's Vicky?" Cade and I say at the same time again. We look at each other and share a chuckle despite the annoyance I feel.

Beckett calls over his shoulder, "Vic!"

A bikini-clad redhead bobbing in the water on a unicorn pool float waves her hand. "Hi!"

I glare at my brother.

He shrugs. "What? We met on the plane and really hit it off."

"Sure you did." I roll my eyes.

Beckett shakes his head, a wide smile on his face. "It's fine. Seriously, you two need to lighten up. How many times have the three of us shared a bed over the years? It's not a big deal. Be happy you have a bed. As I said, I had to work to get you that. And if I were you, I'd get your stuff up there and claim it before Calloway or Dreven wake up and come to their senses."

"Okay, yeah, but we're not twelve anymore, Beck," Cade says.

"So what? Embrace the child in you and have fun. We're on vacation!" He yells the last part, opening his arms wide.

Cade turns to me. "Come on. Let's get our bags up there, at least. I'll keep my stuff there but sleep on the couch."

"Are you sure?" I ask.

"Of course, it's not a problem." He leads the way back into the house.

"Upstairs, last room on the right!" Beckett calls out.

Cade takes both of our bags and makes his way up the stairs. I run my hand along the metal railing as I follow him up the grand spiral staircase.

Much to my relief, the last room on the right is indeed vacant. A four-poster bed sits in the center of the room draped in white linens. Everything about the room screams romantic island escape. The en suite bathroom is pure indulgence, featuring a Jacuzzi tub, a walk-in rain shower, and exquisite marble detailing. Glass containers line the marble countertop, each one filled with a different shade of bath salt. I lift one to my face and breathe in the lavender salts.

"Everything okay?" Cade rests his shoulder against the frame of the bathroom's entrance.

"Yeah, I think I'll be using this tub quite a lot." I set

the jar of salts back on the counter and turn to Cade. "I'm not sure this will be as relaxing as Beck promised." I scrunch my nose.

Cade chuckles. "It will be fine. Promise. Come look at this." He waves me forward.

I follow him to the far wall, where French doors open onto a private balcony overlooking the turquoise waters of the Caribbean Sea.

"Wow. That's quite the view." A sailboat in the distance catches my eye, and I smile, thinking of summers on Lake Michigan sailing with my dad before work became his life.

Cade stands behind me, looking out toward the sea. "If Beck could only save us one room, at least he picked one with a stunning view." My eyes shoot toward him, and he reiterates his earlier statement, "Though I'm sleeping on the couch." His hazel stare holds mine. "We're cool?"

"Yeah." I nod. "We're cool." I take a step back from the balcony and retrieve my suitcase at the foot of the bed. "What should we do first? Swim?"

"Sounds like a plan."

CHAPTER TEN

IRIS

The afternoon breezed by with my butt firmly placed in a lounger by the pool and a book in my hand. It's been a few hours of pure relaxation, which is more than I remember taking in years. I can't remember the last time I read a book for pleasure. I picked up a romance novel with a pretty floral cover at the airport and have been engrossed in it all afternoon. I'm not sure what I expected, but the heated, spicy scenes were a surprise and brought mixed emotions. They're good...real good, and have me feeling all sorts of things, especially down below. Yet therein lies the problem. Getting all hot and bothered with Cade bare-chested in the pool mere feet away isn't good for me.

It makes me want things I can't have.

Beckett was right that the guys would sleep most of the day away. Members of the team and their guests start trickling down around four, many complete with bags under their eyes, looking like they just came from a three-day rave. Admittedly, I'm relieved they partied so hard last night. Maybe tonight will have a more relaxed vibe.

The team's goalie, Gunner Dreven, who has earned the nickname the Beast, ambles onto the patio. He stops beside my lounger. His heated stare travels from my toes and up my body until his soulful brown eyes hold mine. The guy is big and intimidating. He's the biggest guy on the team, both in height and muscle. He's a force, and I'm not sure if his attention scares or excites me, though I'm leaning toward the former.

"Don't even think about it, Dreven!" Beckett calls from the pool. "I know you remember my baby sis."

Gunner grunts and narrows his eyes toward my brother, taking a step away from me. "Feltmore!" he growls. "Do you want to tell me why I woke up in a bed next to Calloway? I don't remember much from last night, but I have a fuzzy memory of you, and I'd bet money this is your doing."

"We may have had a conversation." Beckett takes a sip from his beer.

"Don't fuck with me, Feltmore," Dreven grumbles.

Beckett rests his arms against the side of the pool, looking as smug as ever. "Look. We're short on rooms. You and Calloway offered to share."

"I guarantee I offered no such thing," Dreven states.

"Well, Calloway did, and you were wasted enough not to care. So it is what it is." Beckett shrugs.

Gunner stomps around to the other side of the pool, causing Cade and Beckett to hurry toward the center.

Gunner's voice raises as he starts shouting at my brother. With a smirk and a shake of my head, I return to my book. My brother has a habit of just assuming everything will work out in his favor and not thinking everything through. In truth, things usually do just magically work out for him. Opportunities have always appeared before him, inviting him in with open arms. It can be annoying. As the person who set this week up, he should've made sure that his teammates all had their own rooms.

The shouting fades into the distance and becomes white noise as I scan the page of my book. I can't read fast enough as someone grabs the arm of the female lead, and the hot alpha love interest loses his shit. This is literary gold.

"Good book?" Cade stands beside me. I yelp and yank the book to my chest, causing him to laugh. "I guess so."

Noticing the commotion with Gunner has quieted, I peer around Cade to the pool to find my brother making out with...what's her name... Tracy? Stacy? "Everything good?"

"With Dreven? Yeah. He caught wind that the rookie brought six friends. He's on his way to let them know they'll all be sharing the one room."

"Maybe Beck should've made the sleeping arrangements more clear."

"Actual planning?" Cade quirks a brow. "Nah, you know that's not your brother's way. Anyway, you want to help me get the food ready?"

I don't because I know there's always a hot sex scene right after a "touch her and die" scene in a romance book, but I give Cade a nod and close the book. "Let's go."

People are all over the grounds involved in various leisure activities. I've met most players over the years, making many faces I see familiar. I've yet to meet a few of the newer players and of course all the guests. Groups have congregated all over. Some swim. Others are playing golf on the greens beside the house. There are various lounging areas all around, each one containing a group of players and friends. It's pretty cool that they all get to vacation together like this. I'm not sure if all teams are this close, but something I've always admired about the Cranes is how much they seem like a family.

"Baby Sis Feltmore!" Maxwell Park, one of the team's defensemen, waves from the sofa where a handful of people watch ESPN and sports highlights.

A smile forms, and I wave. "Max, you know I hate that name."

"Can't help it, Baby Sis. You know how we are!" He returns his attention to the TV as the announcer recaps a rival team's game last night. Not all teams have their bye week right now, so the guys will no doubt spend a good chunk of their vacation sizing up their opponents.

I turn to Cade. "Why are you all so weird about nicknames? And why does Beckett insist on introducing me as his Baby Sis? It's weird at this point."

Cade chuckles, opening the fridge. "It's just how it is." He pulls out a platter of ribeye steaks. "I'm not a fan of Heartbreaker either, but it's not going to change. Sometimes it's just easier to lean into the madness." He gives me a wink while handing me the platter.

My heart stutters in my chest, and I force my eyes down to the platter of meat. Cade retrieves more food from the refrigerator, and I turn away from him, setting the large plate on the marble countertop.

I clear my throat. "Speaking of the Heartbreaker. Where's your girl for the week?"

Cade nudges my hip with his, setting some food onto the kitchen island. "I have you," he teases.

"Very funny," I quip.

"Well, as you know, not all nicknames are rooted in fact."

Cade's not a liar, yet I don't believe his last statement in the least. He didn't earn his nickname because he sits in the corner and knits sweaters.

I change the subject. "What's on the menu?"

He pulls foil off a metal serving dish. "We had a local woman make us some traditional food from the region. This is called Cou Cou. I guess it's made with corn meal, okra, onion, and butter and is served with flying fish."

"Flying fish?"

"Yeah, Barbados has flying fish."

"No, they don't!" I giggle.

"I'm serious, they do."

I raise a brow, still skeptical.

"We'll go sailing tomorrow, and I'll show you." He grins, making his dimple appear.

"Okay, because that is definitely something I need to see to believe."

We place the trays of catered food in the oven to warm and season the steaks before Cade takes them outside to the grill. I make my way to the living area.

Sebastian Calloway, the team's newest hotshot

center, sees me first. "Baby Sis!" He stands from the sofa and pulls me into a hug. "Glad you could make it! Feltmore said you might be here."

He releases his hold on me. "Good to see you, Bash."

I met Sebastian right after he was drafted to the team last year, and I've adored him since. He reminds me so much of my brother—handsome, fun-loving, and carefree. He's a few years younger than my brother and oddly slightly more mature.

"I heard you had an interesting sleeping arrangement?" I grin, tapping his arm.

"Ha!" He shakes his head. "Yeah, I don't think the Beast appreciated it much. Your brother says I volunteered to share a room. I'm not sure that's the case. But I know I'll agree to just about anything when I'm wasted. So I'm thinking I may have been coerced under the influence."

I laugh. "Oh, I'm sure you were. Beckett's sneaky AF."

He shrugs. "It's fine. We got it all straightened out." He nods to the sofa. "You want to watch some hockey highlights with us?"

"Sure." I take a seat beside him as he and the others start booing at the TV when another rival team pops onto the big screen.

I can't help but smile and admit I love this group of people. Beckett was right; I needed this. I haven't obsessed over any part of my life back home since I've gotten here. It's incredible what a change of scenery can do for the soul.

"He sucks!" Bash yells at some player highlighted on the screen.

"Yeah, we hate him!" I yell.

Bash throws his head back in laughter. "That's harsh, Baby Sis!"

"I mean, he sucks!" I shout out again.

"Better." He chuckles with a shake of the head before leaning in and whispering, "But we kind of hate him, too."

"I knew it." I nudge his side.

Beckett's girl, who I now remember is named Vicki, walks up. "Food is ready," she tells the group.

The guys jump up from the sofa and head straight to the kitchen.

She offers me a glass of pinkish-orange liquid. "I made a batch of rum punch. It's real yummy. Do you want some, Baby Sis?"

Standing from the sofa, I take the glass from her. "Thanks, but it's Iris. Don't call me that again... please." I throw the last word in as an afterthought when I see Vicki's face fall.

Everyone has their limits, and I've clearly found one of mine. Note to self: some nicknames are only acceptable when used by cute hockey players. As I make my way into the kitchen, I can't help but notice they surround me.

CHAPTER ELEVEN

CADE

Chivalry isn't all it's cracked up to be. The thought comes to me as my head pounds beneath my skull. That's now three nights in a row that I've barely slept, and I'm reaching my limit. Sleeping on the sofa didn't sound all that bad when I suggested it. But I'm regretting the offer. The floor of anyone's room would've been better.

Iris went up to her room early, a glass of rum punch in one hand and her book in the other. She stated she was exhausted and turning in. I didn't blame her. We'd had a really early morning, and long day of travel and shenanigans. However, sleeping on a sofa in a common place doesn't allow one to go to bed early. After Iris went to bed, what seemed like a whole other day was lived in front of my sleeping spot. There was a lively game of poker, a planking competition with more screaming than such an activity should have, and a late-night viewing of the latest John Wick film.

The sun currently shines in through the floor-to-ceiling windows, the bright rays attempting to burn my corneas through my closed lids. Reaching over my head, I pull a throw pillow from the corner of the sofa and hold it over my face.

A throat clears, and I peer around the pillow to find Iris dressed in tight little jean shorts and her bikini top. "I'm ready for that sail date you promised." She grins like someone who's had a glorious night of sleep.

With a sigh, I toss the pillow away and sit up.

"Oh my gosh! You look miserable." She gasps.

I pin her with a stare. "Thanks?"

She chuckles, putting her hands on her hips. "I'm sorry that came out rude. I'm just saying you look exhausted. You have the biggest purple bags under your eyes I've ever seen."

I nod with a yawn. "I'm pretty damn exhausted."

She holds her hands to her mouth. "Oh, I'm sorry. People were in here all night, weren't they? Ugh, I knew it. I wanted to tell you last night that you were welcome to sleep in my room. I mean, it's not like we haven't shared a bed a hundred times before. I feel like an ass."

I shake my head, or at least I think about doing so. "It's fine. It's not your fault."

"I'm going to make you some coffee." She hurries to the kitchen. "Some strong stuff."

I doze off for a second, waking when I feel Iris near. Peeking my eyes open, I find her standing before me, a mug of coffee in her hand and a worried expression on her face. "We don't have to go. Why don't you go up to my room and get some rest? I'll take a rain check on our sailing day."

I hold out my hand and beckon for the coffee. "No, I'll be fine after some coffee and a shower. Promise."

She scurries off again. "I'll make breakfast."

After several cups of coffee, extremely salty eggs that Iris apologized for repeatedly, and a shower, I've mustered up the energy for another day. We meet Freddy, a guy I found online who rents sailboats, by the dock. Most of the guys were still sleeping when we left, so it's only Iris and I on this excursion. A brief and unnecessary tutorial is completed, then Iris and I are on the water.

I'm not the best sailor, but thanks to Beckett, I can manage. His family was really into sailing when we were in high school. Iris, however, knows her way around a sailboat as good as if not better than Beckett, and I find it sexy as hell.

I take a seat in the back of the boat, plop a sucker in

my mouth, and pull a beer out of the cooler. "I'm just going to let you take the lead," I call out over the wind.

"Works for me!" She smiles. "Can you tighten the sheet on that back winch? It's a little loose. The main sail is slacking."

"Sure." I set my beer down and turn the lever to tighten the cable that people who sail call a sheet for some reason. It's attached to the main sail.

"Thanks!" Iris beams as she takes the wheel and steers the sailboat through the pristine water.

The water is a beautiful teal and the sky a perfect blue. A few fluffy clouds in the sky add to the view. Growing up, this is a life I never dreamed I'd have—vacationing in Barbados with my NHL hockey team, in a mansion, and having the means to rent an expensive boat for a day of sailing. As a boy, this life was so far outside my realm of possibilities, I didn't know to dream for it. And I got it anyway. It's something I never take for granted, not for a second.

"Oh my God!" Iris shrieks, and I follow her line of sight.

Clusters of fish jump out of the water alongside the boat, spreading their wings and gliding through the air beside us. "Told ya!" I chuckle.

"They have wings!" she shouts.

"Flying fish! They're all over these waters. Though

they don't actually fly. It's more of a jump and glide. But they're cool, right?"

"So neat! And so weird." She smiles over her shoulder. The sight makes me swallow hard. She wears her hair in a loose braid. Strands that have broken free whip around her face in the wind. The sun hits her pale skin, and I swear she looks like a goddess. She's so breathtakingly beautiful that it's painful at times.

"You put on sunscreen, right?" I call out.

"Of course. SPF 100." She laughs. "I don't want wrinkles. Did you?" She looks over her shoulder again.

She knows me too well. "I tan."

Puckering her lips, she furrows her brow. "In my bag! Put it on. Sun on the water is more intense. A sunburn will ruin the rest of your week. Trust me."

I do as instructed, though I hate the feel of the stuff on my skin.

We take turns steering the boat as we sail around. The flying fish never become less amusing. We laugh and make small talk. We have a picnic lunch on the boat with some random things we were able to pick up. The day is incredible and feels almost normal between us, like it used to when we were best friends. Before.

Iris steers the boat into the dock, maneuvering it among the other ships in port with precision. She said she hasn't been out sailing in a while, but she's still a pro. We thank Teddy and give him a generous monetary tip for all his help in setting this day up.

What a perfect day it was.

When we arrive back at the house, it's buzzing with action. The property is charged with sounds of fun—music, laughter, and lively chatter.

"Seems the nightly party has already begun." Iris smiles my way.

I set our cooler and beach bag down on the foyer floor as we enter the house. "That it does."

Beckett, with his arm draped around Vicki's shoulders, greets us. "I can't believe you went sailing without us!"

"I tried to wake you up... three times," Iris says.

"Same, bro. You weren't having it. I believe your exact words were fuck off," I add.

Beckett laughs. "Stop with the lies. I have no recollection of that."

"Well, you did," I say.

"You did," Iris agrees.

"I faintly remember that, too." Vicki presses her lips in a line as if she's not sure she should agree with us or not.

Beckett shrugs. "Damn. Well, bummer. Did you all have fun?"

A genuine smile crosses Iris's face. "So much fun. It

was the best day. Did you know that they have fish that fly?"

"Yeah." Beckett nods. "Saw them last time we were here. Well, glad you guys had fun, and I hope you're ready to have some more. A fierce cornhole competition is going on in the back if you want to join. We just came in to restock the drinks."

We follow Beckett out back, where drinks have clearly been flowing freely. It's a much more lively scene than yesterday. Reminds me of a rich kid's spring break party from some cheesy TV show. If I'm not mistaken, more people are here, too.

"I'm not crazy. There are new people here, right?" I ask.

"Oh yeah! Vicki invited some of her friends, and they invited some people. It's definitely helped the guy-to-girl ratio." Beckett shoves a drink into my hand. "We're re-creating Sunday's party tonight since we missed it."

"Great." My response is less than amused.

"Yeah!" Beckett misses the sarcasm in my tone. "One of the local DJs should be here any minute with his equipment. Apparently, he's pretty cool. Some of the girls saw him last night at the club."

"It's our turn." Vicki tugs on Beckett's hand, leading him toward the cornhole boards.

Iris leans in. "I can make you an espresso Martini?"

"Yes," I exclaim, a little too loud. "You read my mind."

She chuckles. "I figured you'd need more caffeine to get through the night."

"Definitely."

"Heads-up, Heartbreaker!" Bash calls.

Raising my hands, I catch the football before it hits my face and throw it back to the guys.

I remove my T-shirt and kick off my flip-flops, leaving me in just my swim trunks. I enter the pool, and the warm water feels nice. I imagine the chlorine cleansing the salt from the sea spray and copious amounts of sunscreen off my skin as I fall into a back float. As much as I loved the day, I don't enjoy the added crap on my skin.

A shadow covers me, and I open my eyes to find Iris entering the pool in her string bikini with a plastic cup in each hand. I stand, and she hands me one.

"Red Solo cup Martini for you! I figured a real Martini glass was asking for trouble with all the balls flying around here." Her cheeks flush, and she stumbles over her words. "I mean, a football and those cornhole bags are flying around, and I swear while I was making these, a golf ball flew by the kitchen window."

I smirk. "Yeah, totally got what you meant, and I agree." I tip my cup toward hers in a cheers. "This is safer."

We make our way across the pool to the side under the shade of a group of palm trees. Leaning against the ledge, we watch as some of the guys toss a neon green football around. "This is good." I nod toward the drink.

"Half caffeine and half booze. There's not a better combo out there." She tilts her head back and takes a big gulp. "The DJ arrived while I was making these. Beck is ecstatic."

"I'm sure he is."

We're silent for a beat until Iris lowers her voice and says, "Thanks for today, Dummy. I know we don't talk as much anymore, so understandably, you wouldn't know, but I really needed it."

I dip my chin. "Yeah, I know, and I'm glad. Just because you don't tell me things doesn't mean I don't see you, Rosie. I've always seen you."

Her cheeks flush again, and I chug the rest of my drink to stop myself from saying anything else.

CHAPTER
TWELVE

IRIS

The DJ is obsessed with songs from over a decade ago, and I'm here for it. Every jam takes me back to my middle school days, and that time in my life was good to me. I vividly remember dancing to Icona Pop's "I Love It" at Beck and Cade's sophomore homecoming. I was in eighth grade at the time, but they snuck me into their high school dance. It was a magical night.

History repeats as the three of us dance in a circle, arms in the air, and scream, "I don't care. I love it." We're completely out of tune but totally in unison.

I'm channeling my inner thirteen-year-old, save for the over-indulgence on alcohol, and embracing her spirit. I was a different person then. Sure, everyone changes as they grow into an adult, but I'm fundamentally different. Before this trip, I'd lost my joy. I followed a set of arbitrary guidelines I'd set up, convincing myself that they were important for some reason. The carefree girl I used to be had been replaced by the exact opposite—perhaps to prove something or protect myself, I'm not sure. What I do know is that she wasn't happy.

I don't have a job, a boyfriend, or a plan, and I can honestly say that the past couple of days have been the best I've had in years.

The song ends, and I excuse myself from the space we've claimed as our makeshift dance floor on the back lawn.

"I'm coming with." Cade jogs up behind me. "Are you getting another drink?"

"No, water. You?"

"Same."

Grabbing two waters from the cooler, I hand one to Cade. "Did I see Vicki kissing the DJ?"

He chuckles. "Yeah. Beck knows. They've apparently moved on. He's been flirting with another girl, too."

"Oh, bummer. I thought their love would last." My sarcasm comes out.

Cade frowns and releases a sigh. "It's sad. Even the greatest loves don't stand the test of time."

"At least they'll always have those three…"

Cade corrects me. "Two."

"Right…two days of unbridled passion." I toss my empty water bottle into the recycling bin. "Hard to believe we've only been here two days. We've packed a lot in."

He finishes his water and tosses it into the bin. "I know," he agrees before releasing a yawn.

"You're exhausted."

"Yeah."

"Me too. It's been a long day. An incredible one but a long one."

He peers over my shoulder at the sectional sofa in the living area. "I think I'm tired enough that I could actually sleep through some of the noise tonight."

I shake my head. "Absolutely not. I told you, you can bunk with me tonight."

"No, it's fine, Iris. Really."

"Cade." I cross my arms over my chest. "I'm not taking no for an answer. You need a good night's sleep, or you'll be a total zombie tomorrow. I have a perfectly good half of a king-sized bed available. There's no reason for you to sleep down here among the chaos. Not to mention, this is supposed to be your week of relaxation, and nothing is rejuvenating about sleep deprivation."

"Are you sure?" His question is hesitant.

"One hundred percent. Come on." I wave him forward. Looking behind Cade, I see Beckett with his new girl. "He's good."

"Definitely won't miss us." The corners of Cade's mouth turn up.

The covers on the four-poster bed are untouched on one side. Only the half I sleep on has the white lines pulled back. "See," I say. "I don't even touch that side."

We brush our teeth at the dual sink and change out of our swimsuits and into sleep attire. I'm sporting a pair of short cotton shorts and a tank, and Cade's in nothing but boxer briefs. I love how guys think boxer briefs are just like shorts, but to me, they're not. They hug in certain places, making the look much more sexy than a pair of sport shorts would be. I try not to focus on his back muscles or tight ass as he hangs up his swim trunks.

I climb under the covers on my side of the bed as Cade does the same. There's a charge in the air, an awareness of something more pressing down against my chest, making my breaths labored.

This is fine. We've had hundreds of sleepovers.

I pull the covers up over my chest. Fisting them beneath my chin, I stare at the ceiling. The repetitive bass can be heard through the walls from the party outside. Yet inside this room, our nervous breaths seem to overshadow everything else.

Cade moves at my side. "What was your favorite part of the day?"

Turning to face him, I find him lying on his side. His stare holds mine. "Um, sailing, absolutely. It's been way too long since I've gone, and I forgot how peaceful it is."

"What'd you think about Dreven's Baka's pasta dish?" he asks.

Gunner made some truffle pasta dish that his grandmother back in Croatia always makes. It was fun seeing all six foot five of him in the kitchen preparing an authentic pasta dish from scratch.

"It was amazing."

"Wasn't it? Everything he's ever made has been fantastic," Cade says.

"He cooks for you guys a lot?"

"No. Maybe twice a year, usually at a get-together like this. But I know he cooks a lot at home. He'll often bring packaged meals he made when we go on the road. He's intense about nutrition."

I grin. "You know, that's what's so fun about being here...getting to see the guys off the ice. It's fun seeing everyone's personalities come out. I don't normally get to see this side of things."

"Yeah, you really only see their game faces."

"Exactly."

We chat for another hour, apparently forgetting that

we came up here because we were exhausted. "You never told me what your favorite part of the day was," I say after a while.

Cade pulls in a breath. His stare falls to my lips and then back to my eyes. "This. Right here. Talking to you, just the two of us is my favorite part."

"Really?"

"Yeah, really. Remember back in the day, Beckett would crash almost immediately, and we'd stay up chatting for hours."

I smile at the memory. "Yeah, once his head hits a pillow, he can't last more than a few minutes."

"Talking to you was my favorite part of our sleepovers," Cade utters.

My eyes drop to his mouth just as his tongue pokes out to wet his full lips, and it does me in. I squeeze my thighs together. My entire body aches for Cade's touch as my heart rate picks up.

"Rosie girl." His words are a husky whisper. "What are you thinking?"

I swallow hard. "I don't know." My voice cracks.

"Yes, you do. Tell me."

I've had very little contact with Cade for years, and now, after just two days together, I've already fallen under his spell. I want him to touch me and kiss me and make me feel alive. The need is desperate, excruciating. But I've felt it before—right before he kissed me... and then left.

What am I doing?

"Iris..."

"No," I state, my chest rising.

I can't do this. I can't lose everything I've worked to overcome.

Cade appears to want me just as much as I want him, but I've thought that before and was proven wrong. When it comes to this man, I can't read him. My mind is too jumbled with lust that I don't see clearly. It's the only explanation.

The last time we kissed destroyed parts of me that have never recovered. The past two days have felt like before, back when we were close. I've missed us. Why would I destroy the friendship we're recovering for a simple touch? It doesn't add up. Yet I want it so much.

Cade pulls his bottom lip into his mouth and scoots closer to me. His hand reaches out and rests on my hip. "Tell me what you want."

"I can't." Emotion clogs my throat.

"Why?"

Because you'll leave and break my heart again.

But I don't say that. I don't say anything. I just stare at his gorgeous face. My breaths become more ragged as I imagine what it would be like to finally touch him.

Realization dawns. I'm an adult. I'm no longer the

sixteen-year-old girl whose identity is wrapped up in a boy. I'm a successful woman who wants to feel good. Even if he walks away again, it shouldn't matter because I'm a different person now. He can't crush me again because I'm in control this time. It's my choice.

Put it off to the alcohol or the intense desire coursing through my veins but my logic seems sound. I'm choosing this because I know whatever tomorrow brings will be fine. He can't break what's already been broken.

"I want you to touch me," I admit.

"Fuck yeah," Cade groans. Not wasting any time, he presses his mouth against mine as he pulls our bodies together.

His lips are soft and firm as they move against mine with precision. His tongue licks across my lip, requesting access, and I give it eagerly. When I open my lips, he slides his tongue in, and I groan into his mouth. Our tongues entwine together as our lips move.

Cade's arousal is hard against my thigh, making me so wet. I ache with need as I swing my top leg over him and press my core against the front of his body, desperate for some relief. He threads his fingers through my hair, pulling me closer as his mouth devours mine. He's ravenous, desperate for me. I know exactly how he feels because I feel the same. I need him everywhere. I want every part of his skin to touch every inch of mine.

I break the kiss and pull my tank top over my head. Cade's face is pained, his pupils dilated as he stares at my breasts. "Iris…" he chokes out.

Reaching under the covers, I remove my panties and shorts and toss them to the side of the bed. "I want to feel you against me." I splay my hands over his chest and run them down his abs until I reach the waistband of his boxer briefs. He assists me in tugging them off.

Covers pulled back, we stare at each other's naked forms. Chests heaving. Breaths heavy. Cade is perfectly irresistible as I always knew he would be.

"Iris," he breathes as he reaches forward and cups my breasts. "I want to kiss every inch of you."

"Then do it." My head falls back as he pinches my nipples between his fingers.

Cade crawls over my body, and I lie back against the bed. On all fours, he kisses up my neck and to my ear. I moan as his lips work their magic over my skin. He wasn't lying when he said he wants to kiss every part of me. His hands smooth over my skin, burning me with their touch as his lips caress, nip, and pull. He sucks on my nipples, and I squirm, needing more. He reads my mind and kisses down my torso, over my belly, and down my thigh all the way to my toes. It's simultaneously delicious and maddening.

He starts working his mouth back up my legs and trails his tongue along my inner thigh. Unabashedly, I open my legs, letting my knees fall to the side. Cade hisses and stares between my legs. I prop myself up on my elbows and watch as he slides a finger inside me. His mouth is slack as he breathes heavily. His eyes are dark as his muscled form rests between my legs. His heated stare causes me to breathe heavier. His expression is carnal, and I want him inside me. I want to feel every inch of him pound into me again and again.

I whimper as he inserts a second finger and starts moving. "Ahh," I whine as he works his fingers in and out, running them along my clit. "Cade." I sigh, falling back onto the pillow.

His mouth covers my bundle of nerves, and his tongue starts moving as his fingers work over my G-spot. I'm panting and whining, completely out of my mind with sensation, and I don't care as I let it out. Reaching down, I grab his hair and thrust myself into his mouth over and over as his tongue continues its delicious assault. "I'm gonna…" I moan as my climax rises, screaming as my orgasm hits. Every nerve in my body erupts, and my body explodes with euphoria. I see stars behind my eyelids as wave after wave of pleasure courses through me.

Holy shit.

My mind and body are jelly as Cade kisses his way back up to me. "Good?" He presses his lips to the side of my throat.

I trail my fingers down his back. "So good."

Cade lies beside me and circles his arm around my waist, pulling me close. He kisses my shoulder and leans his head against mine.

"Do you have a condom?" I ask when I catch my breath.

His fingertip traces circles around my belly button, causing my skin to pebble with goose bumps.

"Don't need one. Tonight was about you." He pulls my back against his front. Reaching down, he lifts the covers over our bodies and wraps his arm around me. He splays his hand on my stomach, holding me close to him. With another kiss on my shoulder, he says, "Good night."

I want to press for more. If Cade is that good at oral sex, I can't imagine how good he is at the real deal. But I'm too sated and exhausted to protest. "Night." I place my hand over his as sleep pulls me under.

CHAPTER
THIRTEEN

CADE

I ris's body is soft up against mine. Her back rises and falls in sleep as visions of last night flash through my mind. I'm having a hard time processing the fact that it happened. I've wanted to touch Iris since hormones emerged at the age of twelve. A good amount of energy has been spent for over half my life trying *not* to touch her. Ghosts of my past insecurities linger, and the familiar anxiety that I fuck things up threatens to surface. I will them down. Nothing will ruin the experience with Iris last night. I won't let it.

Quietly, I slide off the bed and head into the bathroom, where I turn on the shower. A glance at my cell tells me it's almost noon. Best sleep I've had in a long time. I feel great. Sure, the days of sleep deprivation or the excess of alcohol and sun I consumed yesterday may have contributed to the most blissful night of sleep I've had in years, but I'd like to believe that was all her. I know it was. A dream come true.

Now, what the dream means for today, I'm not sure. Expectations aren't something I can afford to put a lot of stock in because I have no idea where Iris's head is. We've been virtual strangers for years while she was supposedly happy and with that lawyer guy. Not having a view into that relationship, I can't say how broken up she is about it. For all I know, last night could've been a rebound. If it was, I'll take it and be happy we're talking again. I've missed her.

Not to mention, this luxurious island life will only last a few more days, and then I'm traveling with the team while she's… figuring her life out.

Dipping my head beneath the warm spray of the shower, I rinse the shampoo from my head and conclude that I'll play it cool and leave the ball in her court. I'll follow her lead today and see where it goes.

I quickly dry off, get dressed, brush my teeth, and sneak out of the room without disturbing Iris. Downstairs, I find Beckett flipping through channels on the television with a bottle of water in his hand.

"You're up early," I say.

He looks over his shoulder. "Dude. I had the best sleep. You know how sometimes you can have these amazing drunk sleeps where you sleep like a rock and wake up refreshed?"

"Yeah."

"That was last night. I'm ready to go today."

"Good. I figured you would've gone to bed a few hours ago."

He tilts his head to the side. "Honestly, I don't remember. I think I went up around five."

"And Vicki?" I walk around the sofa and take a seat at the end.

Beckett rolls his eyes. "Don't even get me started on that one."

"So she left with the DJ?"

"No, bro. She's in the rookie's room with him and all his friends. I don't even know. Don't care. So what's the plan today?"

I shrug. "Lying around the pool eating and drinking?

He holds his fist out for me, and I bump it with mine. "Perfect plan, my man." His brows pinch together. "Where did you end up, by the way? I figured I'd find you down here on the sofa."

"Iris offered up half of her bed. Said it was big enough to share."

He nods. "Gotcha. Cool. Glad you found a bed."

"Yeah, me too. I needed it."

Beckett and I get sucked into a classic Sandra Bullock movie as the others start trickling down the stairs in various degrees of hungover, ready to start the day.

"*Miss Congeniality*! We loved this movie." Iris joins us, wearing another bikini top and a pair of shorts.

I watch her for signs and can't read her. She makes coffee and offers cups to everyone who wants one before sitting between Beckett and me, holding her mug of coffee. I wait for a stolen glance or any nonverbal communication that would give me a clue as to what last night meant for her, but no such clues come. This is why I've avoided relationships. Not that one night signifies a relationship, but still. It's frustrating and confusing, and I find myself second-guessing everything. This situation makes me feel naive and juvenile, and in all honesty, I hate it. I don't like putting myself in situations of uncertainty. Chalk it up to years of trauma or whatever but I need to know where I stand.

Abruptly, I stand from the sofa. "I'm going to go for a run."

"What?" Beckett scoffs. "It's like a hundred degrees."

I don't bother answering him. Hurrying up the stairs to the bedroom, I pull a pair of socks and tennis shoes from my bag and slip them on. I have an overwhelming desire to run until I can't feel anything because it beats feeling like this.

The door to the bedroom closes, and Iris stands before me. "What's wrong?"

"Nothing."

"Why won't you look at me?" she asks.

Snapping my head up, I hold her stare. "Just tying my shoe."

"Stop, Dummy. Don't make this weird." She sighs.

I stand with a huff. "What?"

"We're adults. We fooled around, and now today, you sneak out of bed and won't even look at me. I get it. You regret it. Just like before. Only this time, we're stuck together in this house, and there's nowhere for you to run." She looks down at my feet. "Only there is."

I open my mouth to speak, but I'm at a loss for words.

Iris continues. "It doesn't have to be like this, okay? We won't do it again. Problem solved. I feel like I just got you back in my life, and now you're running again. It's stupid. I don't want to return to forced conversations and awkward silences when we're around each other. I thought you were into me, but clearly, I misread you. I've never been able to read you correctly. But last night took two people, Cade. No one made you do anything you didn't want to do. Just man up and move on."

My mouth falls open, and I look at her in confusion. "You think I regret it?"

She crosses her arms over her chest. "Well, obviously. You're literally running away from me."

"I don't regret it," I state.

"You don't?"

"No, do you?"

She shakes her head. "No."

"Then why are we fighting?"

She scoffs. "Because you're ignoring me."

"I'm not ignoring you, Iris. I left the room quietly because I didn't want to wake you. And I looked at you for some sort of sign when you came downstairs, but you didn't give me anything."

"What was I supposed to say? Hey, Cade! Thanks for the amazing orgasm last night! Oh, I love Sandra Bullock!" She puts her hands on her hips. "Where was the opportunity for discussion in that scenario?"

I throw my head back and laugh. "I'm sorry. I suck at this."

"Yeah, you do."

"So what now?" I ask.

"We should talk, Cade. What do you want? What was last night to you? Was it a one-time thing? Do you want to do it again?"

I lower my stare and take a step forward. "Oh, I want to do it again."

"Really?"

"Of course. Do you?" I take a few more steps until I stand so close I can see the darker specks of blue in her bright eyes.

Her back is pressed against the door, and she simply says, "Yeah, I do."

Taking her chin between my thumb and forefinger, I tilt her face up to mine. She breathes heavy as her stare jumps between my lips and eyes. Unable to wait another second, I kiss her. And fuck me if it's not even better sober. She threads her fingers through the hair at the nape of my neck and pulls me close. Our tongues dance, and our lips kiss hard and punishing.

We're a pair of moans and pleas for more. I position my thigh between her legs as I hold her against the door. She starts moving against my leg, and it's enough to make me want to lose it. We kiss until my lips ache. Needing her to come undone the way she did last night, I unbutton her jean shorts and slide them to her ankles. Moving the fabric of her bikini bottoms to the side, I slide a finger into her wet entrance as a collective moan sounds.

"Fucking A," I moan against her mouth as I add another finger. She whimpers, and it makes me painfully hard and needy. At this moment, I'd give up everything to spend the rest of my days between her legs. She drives me to insanity.

I slide two fingers in and out of her warmth, my thumb giving attention to her clit. She rides my hand as her tongue slides in and out of my mouth, mirroring the movements below. Her moans get louder, and she digs her fingers into my shoulders as she all but fucks my hand harder and harder.

"Cade..." My name trembles from her lips.

I continue my assault below and close my mouth around her nipple. I suck as she trembles.

"Cade!" she calls out right before she falls over the edge, her body convulsing and tightening around my fingers. I move my hand until her tremors stop.

Kissing down her body, I drop to my knees, needing to taste her.

"What are you doing?" she exhales.

Replacing my fingers with my mouth, I lick up the evidence of her release. My body is on fire, high on Iris. I lift one of her legs and drape it over my shoulder, opening her wide for me. With one hand, I hold her swimsuit to the side, and I open her for me, using two fingers. My other hand re-enters her body as my tongue works against her bundle of nerves.

"Cade." She runs her fingers through my hair. "What are you doing? I can't..."

I don't know what I'm doing, only that I need her. Every part of her. My breaths are ragged as I lick, taste, and suck.

"Oh my God," she cries out, the sound almost pained as she pulls at my hair. "Ohh..." She starts moving against my mouth, and I know she has another one in her. She whines as her body starts shaking, and then she's coming again.

My tongue moves against her until she's still. I reposition her bathing suit and kiss up her body until I stand. She drapes her arms over my shoulders and leans her face against my chest. "You're going to kill me, Cade Richards. Death by pleasure."

"Oh, what a way to go." I kiss the top of her head.

"You're not going to run, are you?" she asks.

"No running."

"And we're doing that again tonight?"

I chuckle. "Fuck yeah, we're doing that again."

She stands tall and looks up at me. "So what does this mean? What are we doing here?"

"What do you want?" I ask in all sincerity even though I'm aware it sounds like a cop-out.

She bites her bottom lip and looks off to the side. After a beat, she returns her stare to me. "Let's just have a good time this week, and we'll figure it out later. We're on vacation, and we're having fun. Right?"

I nod. "Okay. And your brother?"

She furrows her brow. "Not a word to my brother."

"Deal."

CHAPTER
FOURTEEN

IRIS

The majority of us sit in the pool while Beckett stands on the patio and goes on about the bottle of alcohol in his hand. "Now, gold rum gets its color from aging in barrels or sometimes the addition of caramel. It has a richer and more complex taste than the white rum I just talked about, but its flavor is still smooth enough to make it a good addition to mixed drinks and is one of the most popular rums used to mix in cocktails."

"Boo!" the team's equipment manager, Eddy, catcalls. "Who is this loser!"

"Shut your face," Beckett snaps back and turns to the girl helping him with his rum presentation. She's filled up a tray of plastic cups with a shot's worth of the gold rum. "Go ahead and pass them out, babe, to everyone but that dick." He points at Eddy.

"Come on, Feltmore. I'm just kidding. I want to try the gold!" Eddy protests from the pool.

"Aw, fine." Beckett shoots Eddy a grin. "You know I can't stay mad at you, bud." He looks at the blonde with the tray of drinks. "He's cool, babe."

"What's Beck's current girl's name?" I ask Cade.

"Hell if I know. I doubt he even knows. That's probably why we've only heard him call her babe."

"True." I chuckle.

Babe hands me a cup of the gold rum, and I thank her. Tilting my head back, I take the shot for the second time today. A group of us walked around the city earlier to do a little sightseeing, and somehow, we ended up on a rum taste-testing tour. This guy named Dwight, the rum tour guide, spotted us from a mile away, I'm sure. He was a great salesman and reeled us in with a few sentences. Beckett was in the moment he said rum. It was actually tons of fun. Apparently, Barbados is known for its rum. Dwight was hilarious, energetic, and had a great teaching style. It didn't hurt that we tasted each rum as we learned about it. He made the history of rum so interesting. So much so that Beckett bought a bottle of all the rum varieties we sampled to bring back so he could enlighten the rest of the crew about the miracle that is rum.

"Better than the white! More flavor." Max holds up his plastic cup. Babe hurries over and retrieves it.

"Right? I thought so, too," Beckett says as he starts preparing the next bottle for tasting.

Cade releases an amused huff. "Your brother is something else."

"Your best friend is something else. He's always the center of attention"—I wave my hand through the air —"and the life of the party. Has that ever bothered you?"

"Nope. I'm glad that's Beck's thing so it doesn't have to be mine. I've never needed fame or the attention."

"Says the millionaire professional hockey player," I tease.

He shrugs. "I started playing because your brother wanted me to. I found I was pretty good, and it was something to do. Once it was time for college, I couldn't think of any other options at the time."

"You don't regret it, do you?"

"No, of course not. I love it. I mean, I get to skate and play hockey with my best friend every day and make damn good money doing so. I don't regret it at all."

Cade and I are seated at the end of the pool, where it has a built-in ledge under the water. It's my favorite place in the pool to relax. The water reaches just above my waist, and my legs dangle off the ledge into the deeper water. This section of the pool is beneath a line of palm trees and is always in the shade. It's the perfect relaxation spot.

Beckett enthusiastically gives the history and attributes of spiced rum. He's no Dwight, but I have to admit, he's a close second. It's really no surprise that he could moonlight as a rum tour guide since there's nothing my brother can't do.

Babe carries her tray of cups, now with spiced rum, around to the group.

I take the cup from her and swish the rum in my cup. Leaning in, I give it a smell. "Do I detect a note of cinnamon, nutmeg, and vanilla?"

Cade quirks a brow with a smirk. "I don't know what you're smelling. Mine smells clearly of basil and cilantro."

I nudge his side with a laugh before drinking down the spiced rum. I shake my head after swallowing. "That one burned a little."

"Is it me, or are they all starting to taste the same?" His face scrunches as he swallows the cup of straight alcohol.

"Totally! That could be from the fact we're still tipsy from the original tasting."

"True. Dwight was a heavy pourer."

When Babe comes by with cups of the overproof

rum which is twice the alcohol content, Cade and I both decline. I have no intention of passing out tonight. I'm officially rummed out.

Beckett holds up a glass bottle in each hand. "Let's review…"

"What in the hell is he going on about?" I grimace, my head feeling fuzzy.

Cade pulls me up so I sit on his lap, and he traces his fingers up and down my back. "He's drunk with power."

"Literally." I giggle.

His hands dip below the water, and he glides them along my back, thighs and legs.

"Cade," I warn under my breath.

"No one can see anything. Trust me."

Beckett continues talking on the patio on the other side of the pool. "I will give the first person who can correctly identify the traditional, aged, white, black, spiced, overproofed, and gold rum a thousand dollars." Half the pool occupants rush toward the steps to join Beckett on the patio. "By taste alone! Meaning you'll be blindfolded."

An excited round of "easy," "piece of cake," and "get your money ready, Feltmore" sounds around the patio as the guys circle Beckett and Babe as they prepare the competition cups.

Cade uses the distraction to slip his hand into the front of my bikini bottoms. I gasp.

"No one is going to see, but you have to be quiet." He nips at my ear.

His fingers start working their magic against my clit while he slides his other hand under my thigh, beneath my bathing suit, and inserts two fingers inside me. His hands work beneath the water in an incredible assault. I bite my lip and breathe in through my nose, reining in my noises. I want to tell him to stop and head somewhere private, but the fact that we're out in the open with other people makes the sensations more intense.

"You getting close?" His heated breath warms the back of my neck.

I nod, afraid of opening my mouth.

He works me higher and higher. I grip his forearms and hold on tight. The prickles form on my skull, and my skin warms as it prepares for the impending sensations.

Cade's fingers move in and out while his others move back and forth in a perfect rhythm. I'm falling over the edge, drowning in ecstasy. The loud moan escapes before I have the chance to stop it.

And then he shoves my head underwater. Startled, I suck in a gulp of water. Lifting my head from the water, Cade splashes me in the face as I cough up the water from my lungs.

"Stop drowning Baby Sis, and get over here and join the competition!" Beckett calls out.

"Can't," Cade answers. "We're still drunk from earlier. They all taste the same at this point."

"Lame," Beckett says.

I take hold of Cade's wrists and yank him from the underwater bench, and then I climb up his body trying to pull his face beneath the water, but he doesn't budge. "You asshole."

"You didn't leave me much choice." He laughs as I splash his face with water.

"That hurt! There's water up my nose and in my lungs," I grumble, hitting my palms against his chest.

He holds his hands out to shield his face as I splash more water toward him. "Did you want me to let the whole team hear you come? Did you want Beckett to hear you?"

I halt my water assault. "No," I grumble.

"Well, then?"

"I guess you're right."

"Plus, it was your fault for crying out like that." He playfully pokes my belly.

"My fault?" I scoff, quirking a brow. "I'd say it's your fault for starting the whole thing."

Cade laughs, and I'm hit with a wave of awe at just how beautiful this man is and how desperately I want him.

"Come on," I say.

Moving through the water, I start up the ladder. "Where're we going?"

I press my finger to my lips. "Shh."

He shakes his head. "Okay, then. Lead the way."

Leaving the others on the patio distracted by Beckett's game of *Guess the Rum*, I make my way around the posh cabana that functions as a poolside bar and grill. Once we're out of sight, I take hold of Cade's hand and pull him into the bathroom at the back of the building. The room is on par with the rest of the estate in its luxury. A crystal chandelier hangs from the vaulted ceiling beneath a large skylight. The sun shines in through the rooftop window and reflects through the clear pieces of the chandelier, causing an almost disco ball effect. Light bounces off the walls, making it feel like we're in some sort of fairyland.

I eye the teal sofa against the wall by the door. "Wait here."

Making my way across the room, I open the top drawer of the vanity. When I was in here earlier looking for more sunscreen, I discovered a box of condoms in the drawer. I retrieve one of the foil packets, return to Cade, and place the little square package in his hand.

He eyes it and lifts his gaze to me. "No, Iris. We are not having sex in here."

"Why not?"

"Because it's a bathroom."

I pout my lips, unamused. "It's the nicest bathroom I've ever seen. Look, there's even a couch far away from all that over there." I motion toward the toilet.

"We're not doing this for the first time here. Okay?" His words are soft as he takes a step toward me. He glides his hands up and down my arms.

"So you want to go up to the room?"

"We can't just disappear in the middle of the day. As soon as your brother's game is over, he'll come looking for us."

"That's true." I sigh. "Fine but that doesn't mean I'm going to leave here empty-handed."

He reaches toward me and grips my waist. I slap his hands away. "No. Don't go touching me and getting me all crazed out of my mind. I'm on a mission."

"A mission?"

I lick my lips, and I splay my hands across his chest with a nod. "You're always taking care of me. I want to return the favor."

Cade releases a groan as I lean forward and flick his nipple with my tongue. I slide my hand down his abdomen and into his swim trunks. He hisses as I grasp his impressive length, already hard for me. "Shorts off."

He complies, sliding his trunks to the ground as I move my hand over him.

"I've wanted to do this all week," I say, dropping to my knees. The truth is, I've wanted to do it for a hell of a lot longer than that.

I take him into my mouth, relishing in the guttural sigh that leaves his lips, and then I work to make him feel as good as he makes me feel.

CHAPTER
FIFTEEN

IRIS

The entire team, save for Gunner and Cade, gathers around the makeshift beer pong table we made by pushing a couple of the tables from the cabana together.

This lively gathering has had us huddled around this long, beer-soaked table adorned with countless red Solo cups for hours. Miraculously, we're all still standing. The current competition finds me and Beckett on one side of the table, squaring off against Bash and Max. I've never had so much fun playing a game where the winner gets... less drunk? This is an ancient battle of skill and precision, though I'm not sure what qualifies as winning. I'm going to go out on a limb and say Beck and I are in the lead because we're slurring our words less than the guys at the other end of the table.

Max places a cup on his end of the table, and Beckett launches the ping pong ball into the air as our friends erupt in cheers. Beckett's arms fly into the air in victory as the ball lands in the cup. He turns in a circle as if he's just won a boxing competition, and everyone goes wild. My laughter at the absurdity of it all brings pain to my stomach, and I hold my sides. My brother is an idiot… and oh, how I love him.

A look over Beck's shoulder finds Cade and Gunner sitting on the underwater ledge at the end of the pool. They lean back against the rim of the pool, their arms outstretched, holding a bottle of beer as they talk. Gunner is a beast of a man and, by all accounts, attractive. Yet something about Cade has always done me in. He outshines every man here. I've always found everything about him, both his physical and personality attributes, utter perfection. He's the most attractive man—I shake my head, clearing that thought. I don't have time to obsess over Cade when I have a game to… win. I don't know what we're doing here.

"Get your head in the game, Baby Sis." Beckett takes me by the arms and gives me a shake.

"I'm sorry. I'm on it." I toss my ball.

"Nice!" Beckett shouts when I land my ping pong ball in the cup. "Drink up!" he says to our opponents.

In my periphery, I can see Cade step out of the pool and make his way over to us.

Bash lands two balls in a row into cups, forcing Beckett and me to drink the disgusting lukewarm beer.

I swallow with a grimace and shake my head. "Ick."

Cade stands behind me and rubs his thumb down my spine, causing me to shiver, the sourness of the beer forgotten. He's been secretly touching me ever since what will always be remembered as my two mind-blowing orgasms against the door moment. Heck, this week will be my insanely epic orgasm era. I can't honestly say I've ever been so completely satisfied in my life.

Not that I care to bring up my ex, but sex with him was always hard and fast. It was near instant gratification for him and, sadly, not much for me. He was always too busy to consider my needs. While I'm not in a relationship with Cade, my needs are always his focus. It's a little unsettling because the guy seems to focus only on my pleasure. He won't have sex with me.

I'm trying not to let the fact that the Cranes *Heartbreaker* won't sleep with me get me down. He'll lick me for hours, but it never goes further. It's hard to complain when I'm in a constant state of sated bliss, but I'm starting to wonder what the deal is. I'd say he's taking it slow, but we have been doing anything but.

Yesterday, I stepped into the pantry to get sugar for some drinks I was making for the group. Cade followed me in there and fingered me so deliciously that I came next to the spices in a matter of seconds.

"I'm tapping out," I say to my brother.

"No," he protests.

Gripping his shoulder, I say, "We've been at this for hours. I'm done."

He waves me off and pulls one of the guys in to take my place.

I make my way to the shaded area by the pool and plop my butt onto the cushioned seat of the lounger. My romance book sits unfinished on the table beside me. The relaxing week I thought I was getting has eluded me, but I can't say I'm disappointed. This week has been freeing in so many ways. I've been having too much fun to even think about the shitstorm of a life I have waiting back in Michigan. As busy as I've been here, I've been able to breathe fully for the first time in years. I've barely begun to dissect or make sense of my life back home over the past several years, but the fact that I wasn't in a good mental headspace is glaringly obvious. It only took a week of partying in a mansion in Barbados with an NHL hockey team and a dozen mind-blowing orgasms from my lifelong crush to put it all into perspective.

An underlying current of fear courses through my

veins. To say I'm not nervous about going home would be a lie. Whenever I feel anxious, I look up at the palm trees and push the anxiety down. As long as I'm surrounded by palm trees, I'm still here in this pseudo-universe where my problems don't exist. I'll have plenty of time to fret over my life choices when I return. I'm not going to waste a second of Barbados doing so.

Cade takes a seat in the lounge chair beside me. "Had it with beer pong?"

"God, yes." I nod. "This week has single-handedly made up for all the parties I skipped in college. I'm good. I don't feel like I missed out on anything anymore."

"You didn't do any partying in college?"

"No... I mean, maybe a couple of small get-togethers with classmates a few times, but not really. I was determined to finish law school early so I could start working."

"And you did."

"And I did." I sigh.

"Was it what you thought it would be?" he asks.

I point toward the palm trees overhead.

"Palm trees," he says knowingly, which has become the weekly code word for changing the subject.

The palm tree realization came after the two orgasms against the door moment when Cade wanted to get serious and talk about real stuff. I quickly shut him down, explaining I wanted to be nothing but happy for the rest of the week and talk of nothing serious.

Maybe it's weird, and I should be using this time to figure stuff out, but I'm using this week to recharge so I'll have the mental strength to get my life in order when I return.

And good thing we're in a "palm tree" state because looking at Cade now, I want to discuss everything, which would cast a depressing rain cloud over our last day.

Orgasms aside, this week with Cade has been a dream come true. He's all I wanted since I was young, and for five days, he's been mine. We've snuggled in bed every night and talked for hours about nothing. We've laughed until my sides ached. Beckett's been in host mode all week, so he's all but left us alone, not noticing the increased time Cade and I have spent together.

The truth is, this is what I thought it would be like after the kiss eight years ago. This feels like what we were meant to be. I'm not sure what tomorrow will bring when we have to pack up and fly back to reality. But this week is going to play on the highlight reel in my mind forever.

CHAPTER SIXTEEN

CADE

I'll take ways I didn't see this week ending for five hundred, Alex.

Old reruns of *Jeopardy* play on the big screen in the living room while a mix of laughter and shouting sounds from the kitchen. Because nothing says Barbados like a trivia game show at two in the morning and a group of professional hockey players and Iris hurrying around the kitchen… baking?

This week has been surprising, to say the least. Although, that's kind of the allure of our bye week vacations—we never know what's going to happen, and it's always a blast. This vacation is different from year to year—a new mix of people, a different location, and varied shenanigans that always leave us with stories to talk about for years.

Tonight is our final night. I thought maybe we'd go out with a giant party of some sort. Yet all it took was someone to say they made the best chocolate chip cookies for it to turn into a baking competition. I'm not sure how we got on the topic of cookies, to begin with, but the comment was made, and the next thing I knew, we were calling Ubers and heading to the grocery store for everyone's ingredients. And now there's a full-fledged bake-off taking place. When the cookies are done, there will, of course, be blind taste tests and voting and a declared winner. Every person in the kitchen is certain that their secret recipe is the best recipe. There's no denying that this group is competitive at every single thing we do.

I decided to sit out and watch from the sidelines, which is no sacrifice. My sole focus has been on Iris, and I could look at her all day, every day.

This vacation has been chock-full of pleasant unexpected developments, and my time with Iris has been on the top of that list. Half the fantasies I imagined as a teen when it came to Iris have been fulfilled and then some. Best yet, there's been no guilt save for the part about keeping it from Beckett. But other than that, nothing but good thoughts making me think I'm finally, after all these years, ready for the long haul with Iris.

After twenty-six years of self-doubt, I might just feel like I'm enough and worthy of someone as incredible as her.

Iris has been set on "living in the moment" here and hasn't wanted to discuss anything serious. Therefore, I'm not quite sure what tomorrow, after we leave Barbados and return to the real world, will look like.

"It freaking smells like heaven in here," Beckett says before shouting, "Who is John Lennon?" at the TV. "Seriously, how is that not the answer?" he grumbles.

I pull a sucker from my mouth. "I don't know, man. I was zoned out." I didn't hear the answer in the first place to know what Beck is talking about.

After literal hours, the cookies are baked, plated, and cooled. One of Babe's friends has labeled the plates with the letters A through J, and only she knows which letter belongs to which contestant. Now, we're all standing here with pieces of paper in which we are to judge each cookie with a number one to five rating, five being the best chocolate chip cookie we've ever eaten.

I know that the cookies on the plate labeled with the letter C are Iris's. I've been eating her cookies since I was ten and have the appearance, taste, and texture memorized. So of course I give her a five. Taking sips of milk between cookies to cleanse my palette, I continue trying a cookie from all the plates. When finished, I hand my scorecards to Babe and her friend to tally.

Beckett groans beside me. "Turns out, downing a six-pack of beer before eating ten cookies and drinking four cups of milk isn't the best combo." He splays his hand over his stomach and groans.

"Give yourself a minute, and you'll be fine." I bump his shoulder. "You've had a lot worst combos and have come through with flying colors."

"True." His chest heaves with a quiet laugh. "Remember the street cart hot dog competition in San Antonio?"

"Vividly." I grimace, recalling how much I threw up that night.

Iris joins us. Leaning in, she whispers. "You knew which plate was mine, right?"

"Of course. Letter J. I gave it a 5." Beckett gives Iris a wink.

"What? No. Mine were clearly plate C." She furrows her brows.

Beckett covers his mouth. "Really? I gave those a one."

"What?" she whisper-shouts. "Beck!"

He starts laughing. "God, you're so easy to rile up,

Iris. I knew yours were plate C, and I gave them a five."

She blows out a breath and pins Beckett with an unamused stare before looking at me. "Same."

"Good." She looks over her shoulder at the women still tallying and then back at us. "The J cookies were amazing, though."

"They were. I was serious when I said I gave them a five," Beckett says. Iris swats his stomach. "What? I gave yours a five, but I had to be fair. There were other five-worthy cookies too."

"I guess," she grumbles.

"What's the prize for winning?" I ask.

"Bragging rights, I suppose." Iris shrugs.

"That really is the best prize." Beckett crosses his arms and leans back against the wall. "Can you believe it's already our last night? This week always flies by."

"It does," I agree.

"I know," Iris says. "I wish we had more time."

Beckett smiles. "I knew you'd have a ball. I'm glad you finally agreed to come to one of these."

"Yeah, me too. You were right," Iris says.

Beckett scoffs. "Obviously. Always am."

Iris opens her mouth to protest when the women announce they've finished tallying the results. We all gather around the kitchen island.

"Okay, so in third place is plate C, which belongs to Baby Sis." Babe looks at Iris with a smile while we clap.

Iris's face falls. "Thanks," she mutters, less than amused.

"In second place is Max with his cookies from plate A."

Everyone claps.

"And the winner of the Barbados Bye Week cookie bake-off is plate J, which is Bash!"

Bash pumps his fist in the air. "Ha! Suckers. The secret is to use mini-chocolate chips and to double the amount of chips suggested in the recipe. Oh, and to undercook them so they're nice and chewy."

The remainder of cookies on the J plate are snatched up as people hurry to get another taste of the winning cookie.

"Lame." Iris rolls her eyes. "I'm going to bed." She takes off toward the stairs.

Looking down at my phone, I note the time. "Yeah, we have to be at the airport in three hours. I think it's going to be more of a cat nap."

"What's the point of going to bed now?" Beckett questions.

"Exhaustion." I chuckle. "A nap is better than nothing. I'm going to head up, too."

Beckett groans and leans against the wall with his arms crossed. "It sucks that bye week is over.

Though, I am looking forward to getting back on the ice."

"Yeah, me too," I say in all honesty.

"Plus"—he shrugs—"I'm sure it will be nice to have your own bed back and not have to share with Iris anymore."

I nod. "Oh, absolutely."

He hits my arm. "See you in a few hours."

"Yeah. Night."

I feel like death. Okay, maybe that's a bit of an exaggeration, but I don't feel great. Since returning from Barbados three days ago, I've caught a bug, a nasty cold of some sort. Half the team has it. Exhaustion paired with excessive drinking, eating like shit, and traveling through germ-infested airports has allowed a dozen of us to pick up the wannabe plague. Come to think of it, this happens every year.

The locker room is quiet as we dress for the game. The usual shit-talking and humor are absent.

Beckett blows his nose. His eyes are bloodshot as he addresses the team. "We need to rally and get our shit together. Coach is going to be pissed if we play like shit because we partied too hard last week. You know how much he hates our bye week vacation. So suck it up and get mad. We're not losing in Chicago."

The guys start to yell, grunt, and holler random shit about our opponents.

The Blackhawks are one of our rivals, and a win against them would be ideal.

Our head coach, Marcus Albright, enters the locker room. "That's what I like to hear!" He claps his clipboard and nods. "First game back. At least you sound ready. But are you ready?" he yells.

"We're ready, Coach!" the team shouts.

"Alright, get close!" Coach begins his pre-game talk as we all huddle in.

At the back of the huddle, I finish tying my skate. Beckett is right. I need to get my head in the game because it's definitely not. I can't stop thinking about Iris.

Things feel unresolved between us. She was asleep before I finished brushing my teeth the last night of vacation. When the alarm went off three hours later, we had to hurry. We had time enough to throw our stuff in our bags and rush to the airport. There have been a few generic texts since—*made it home, had a great time, good luck this week*—since returning, but nothing of substance. Thanks to her palm tree rule, there was no discussion of anything serious while we were there either.

I don't like this feeling of uncertainty. It opens up all sorts of long buried insecurities that I haven't felt in years. *Up in the air* isn't something I do well. I work in absolutes. We're together, or we're not. Whatever it is we're doing or did in Barbados doesn't have set parameters, and that needs to be resolved soon.

Coach finishes his spiel, and everyone gets fired up.

Hurrying to my locker, I pull out my phone and text Iris.

I miss you.

I hit send and toss my phone back in my locker. Grabbing my gloves, I follow the guys out of the locker room. Chicago's team has a couple of notorious hotheads. I'm actually hoping they start something on the ice. A heated fight against the boards and some time stewing in the penalty box might just be the medicine I need.

The moment the brisk air of the arena hits my skin, a sense of calm comes over me. The cold that has been the bane of my existence for the past three days seemingly disappears. Worries over my love life, or lack thereof, no longer occupy my mind.

Breathing in the cool air brings a sense of purpose. The cheers and even the boos of the opposing team's fans ignite the fierce competitor within. The slicing of my skate blades against the ice causes my mouth to turn up into a smile. The second I move over the ice, nothing else matters but giving everything I've got—and hopefully winning.

Beckett skates toward me and holds out his gloved hand. I bump it with mine. "Barbados was nice, but nothing beats this, does it?" His grin is infectious.

I return his smile. "Sure doesn't, brother. Nothing beats this."

CHAPTER
SEVENTEEN

IRIS

Mom walks across the room. Holding her planner with one hand, she writes furiously in it with her other. I've never met someone who can look both flawless and completely frazzled at the same time.

"Big day, Mom?" I sip my coffee from the comfort of the sofa.

She looks up startled as if she forgot I was here. "Oh, yes. Meetings all day long."

I've never understood how my mother is so busy for someone who doesn't hold a paying job. She volunteers or heads committees and organizes charities. I've been without work for three weeks, and I'm finding it difficult to remove my butt from this couch. Admittedly, the week before my parents' anniversary party, I scurried around much like my mother is now. Maybe the apple doesn't fall too far from the tree.

"You know you can put all that information into your phone, and it'll save you having to write and walk." I give her a smile.

She waves her pen-holding hand through the air. "I prefer a paper calendar. Something is so satisfying about physically checking off items after you've completed them."

"Yeah, I get that."

"So what are your plans today?" she asks.

Turning toward the window, I watch the flurries fall from the gray sky. "I don't know."

She stops moving and faces me. "You know, one word to your father, and you're hired at his firm. He's just waiting for you to ask."

"I know he is. He's been waiting since I graduated from law school."

"So what's the holdup? You'd have fun working with your dad, and he'd love it."

"Fun?" I scoff. "Have you met the man you're married to?"

She narrows her eyes. "He can be fun... in his own way."

"Only if his own way is another way to say completely dull."

"Iris," Mom chastises. "You can't just mope around forever. You planned our party. You went on vacation and spent time with your brother. It's time to move on with your life. Whatever happened at your old firm between you and Ben is over now. Don't let it steal any more of your life from you by wasting your days away."

I sigh. "I've been home four days, Mom. Let's not be dramatic. Sometimes it takes a little bit of time to figure out the next steps."

"Not when the next step is right in front of you. You've done your own thing, proved yourself or whatever. Now, go work with your dad. It's where you were always meant to be anyway."

"I'll figure it out."

"Okay, good. Now." She looks down at her calendar. "I'm going to be gone all day, and then your dad and I have a charity banquet. So you'll have to get dinner on your own."

"I think I can manage."

"Also, when the movers dropped off your stuff, they kind of just placed it everywhere. It's really bugging your father. Maybe you could organize that a bit?"

I pin my mom with a stare. "Seriously? He doesn't even use that side of the garage, which is why I told the movers to put my things there in the first place. It was empty."

She raises her hands. "You know he doesn't like clutter. Just see what you can do, please?" She blows me a kiss and scurries away, face down in her planner.

Coffee cup in hand, I make my way to the oversized four-car garage attached to the house. At the end of the large space sits all my belongings I had moved out of Ben's house while I was in Barbados. I didn't have much there in the first place. Ben's apartment was fully furnished when I moved in with him. Most of these boxes contain clothes or other random personal items. There can't be more than a dozen boxes, and it's annoying my father?

Please.

I set my cup of coffee on the back work counter. Years old, it still looks brand new as my dad hasn't worked on anything in this garage in his life. Stacking the boxes atop each other in the back corner frees up the space, and a car could easily fit now. There were a total of ten boxes, and they bothered my father so much that he had my mom mention it to me.

Yeah, I won't be working with him anytime soon.

I love my dad. I just know that working with him wouldn't be what's best for me. In fact, I'm quite sure it would send me over the edge, and I'd lose my sanity completely. If Barbados gave me anything, it's the realization that it feels good to be happy.

Whatever I decide to do needs to bring me joy. I can't go back to a joyless life.

Leaning against the stack of moving boxes, I finish my now lukewarm coffee and pull out my phone.

I miss you.

The text stares back at me, and I still don't have the words to answer. I know he sent it right before he went on the ice because I watched the game live last night. Getting back to the game after vacation, and I was the last thought on his mind before playing. I don't know how I feel about it.

Do I want him to miss me? I don't know.

Do I miss him? Yeah. Should I? I'm not sure.

Did Barbados Cade bring me joy? Definitely. But that doesn't mean that the real-life version will.

Yet for the first time in a long time, I watched the entirety of a Cranes game. Instead of hoping I wouldn't see Cade on the screen, I looked forward to the times I did. He played beautifully, and his goal helped his team to defeat their rivals. It wasn't the best game the Cranes have played. Their win was aided by the fact that both Chicago's high-scoring center and their starting goalie were out with injuries, and their replacements spent more time in the penalty box than they did on the ice. Yet it was a win nonetheless.

There's no denying the fact that I miss him, too. But we're no longer in the land of flying fish, and as much as I'd like to believe things could be the same here, I'm not naive. The fact is, the trees surrounding me are void of leaves for the winter—there's not a palm tree in sight.

The Cranes game is home tonight. Taking advantage of our season tickets for once, I opt to go. It hasn't even been a week since we left the island, and I miss all the guys. The team has always been kind to me as the great Beckett Feldmore's little sister, but something switched in Barbados. I got to know the guys and built actual friendships. Now I understand why the team is so close. They really are a great group of people.

"It's always so exciting, isn't it?" Mom squeezes my arm. It's just the two of us, as Dad had to work late. We're twinning in our navy blue Cranes jerseys with the bold white number eighteen, Beckett's number.

"It is," I agree as the puck is dropped, momentarily feeling bad that neither of us represents Cade and his number ten jersey. But with a quick scan, I see several women in number ten jerseys, so I don't feel bad. The Cranes Heartbreaker is definitely loved. He'll be just fine.

The Dallas Stars center gains control and rushes into the offensive zone. Hitting the puck to left wing forward, he lines up the shot and the puck flies toward the net before our defensemen can stop it. Mom holds my arm tighter as Gunner Dreven lunges. With a bent knee, he drops to the ice and stops the puck with his glove.

"Nice save, Gunner!" I cheer, clapping my hands.

He hits it to Beckett, and Mom and I jump up and down in front of our seats, screaming for Beck. He hits the puck to Cade, who slaps it back, missing the opponent's defenders. The two of them have always played so in sync. Beckett takes the shot, and it slides under the leg of the Stars goalie.

The crowd goes wild. Mom and I hug each other and jump up and down.

Despite the almost immediate goal after the start of the game, the score remained one to zero until the third period when, with an assist from Beck, Cade scored a goal, bringing the final score to 2-0. Cranes win.

I walk my mom to the car and drive her out of the cluster of traffic after a home game. When we've cleared the bumper-to-bumper traffic, I call an Uber to come pick me up. Once the Uber arrives, Mom continues home, and I head back to the bar the team has rented out for the night. A home game is always followed by a celebration in a local bar.

When I get back, the guys are already there. The place is packed with fans. I run into some of the guys, each one happy to see me, as I make my way through the space in search of Beck and Cade.

I stop, spotting Cade first.

He's leaning up against a tall table, beer in hand, talking to a couple of beautiful women. I want to turn away and go find my brother, but I can't. Instead, my eyes are glued to Cade as he talks, and the girls laugh like he's the funniest person in the world. The brunette places her hand on his forearm as he continues speaking. The blond friend leans in and whispers something in Cade's ear, this time causing him to laugh.

I am not amused. In fact, my stomach feels ill.

Cade "the Heartbreaker" Richards. What did I expect to see? Of course he's going to be flirting with women. There's a reason for his nickname. And why shouldn't he? We never set any expectations beyond Barbados. In fact, I refused to talk about anything serious that week. Heck, I've left his latest text on read for two days, refusing to even text back. I can't be mad that he's talking to other people.

But I am.

A strong set of arms circles me. "Sis!" Beckett squeezes me in a hug.

I turn in his arms and hug him back. "Great game!"

"Thank you. So glad you could make it. Come on." He tugs at my hand. "Guess who else made it up for the game?"

"Who?"

"Amelia." He motions toward the bar.

I have no idea who Amelia is, but when I spot Babe, elbows on the bar and a Martini in hand, it all makes sense. "Ah... Babe," I say more to myself than anyone.

"What?" Beckett asks.

I shake my head and look over my shoulder, wanting to tell Cade that Babe has a name. But he remains across the bar and is still in conversation with the same two women, oblivious to my presence.

"Iris!" Amelia pulls me into a hug.

"It's good to see you again, Amelia." Her name sounds so foreign, and it doesn't fit her at all. "I didn't know you lived in Michigan."

She shakes her head. "I don't. I live in Florida, but I missed my Becky-boo, and I couldn't wait to visit," she says in a baby voice as she wraps her arms around my brother.

Remembering that Amelia was his vacation fling for only the second half of the trip means that she went from meaningless hookup to Becky-boo in less than a week. Yeah, she's not going to last.

Beckett wears a tight smile as Amelia squeezes her arms around him, and I have to stop myself from laughing. Honestly, I don't feel bad for the guy. He gets himself into these predicaments. But seeing as I need someone to talk to, and it won't be Cade, I save him.

"Amelia, do you mind if I have a little time alone with my brother? I'm having a bit of a life crisis and need to talk to him."

Amelia's eyes go wide, and she looks from Beckett to me. "Oh, yeah… sure. I'll be over with Nina at the pool table when you're done." She presses a kiss to Beckett's lips and leaves with a shy wave in my direction.

My brother raises a brow. "Life crisis? Nice save."

I roll my eyes. "I actually am having a life crisis, which is the only reason I saved you. You have to get better at communication when it comes to your hookups."

"I know." He sighs. "It's a problem. But, for real, what's wrong?"

Avoiding the jealousy over Cade conversation completely, I tell him about work. "So I've been home for several days, you know, and our parents expect me to go work for Dad, but the thing is, I really don't want to. And it's not only the fact that I don't want to work at Dad's firm… I don't know if I want to be a lawyer at all. Every time I think about going back to law, I feel sick."

"So you don't want to be a lawyer anymore?" He holds up two fingers to the bartender, ordering a couple more drinks.

"I don't think so, but that's crazy, right? I went to years of schooling for a job that I'm just starting to realize I hate? I should just suck it up, right?"

"Hell no." The bartender places a bottle of beer before each of us. "Life is too short not to be happy, Iris. If you don't want to be a lawyer, don't be."

"But I don't have any idea what I want to be, and I can't just sit around Mom and Dad's house all day doing nothing."

He takes a sip of beer. "Well, what makes you happy?"

I shrug.

"Come on." He sits on the stool beside me and turns to face me. "You love to bake. You love to read. You love to plan parties and decorate. You could search on Pinterest all day for ideas and not get bored. Is there anything involving any of those things that you could do?"

I bite my lip. "Yeah, maybe I could be a decorator or party planner or something?"

His eyes light up. "Oh, you know what? We're hiring."

"Who's hiring?"

"The team. I heard Penny talking about it earlier. They're looking for an events manager or something like that to work with Penny and help plan our events, parties, celebrations... stuff like that. That's right up your alley."

"Yeah, but I don't have a degree for that."

"So what? You don't need a degree. You have the talent, and you have me. Let me talk to Penny and see what I can do."

"Are you serious?" I've never thought about being an events coordinator of any kind, but Beckett is right. I'd rock that job. More importantly, it sounds fun. I'm sure it would be a huge pay cut from my law job, but right now, it's more important for me to be happy than be rich.

"Absolutely. Just give me a couple of days. Okay?"

I smile. "Okay. Thanks, Beck."

"Anytime."

CHAPTER
EIGHTEEN

CADE

I sit in the weight room, beads of sweat glistening on my forehead, my muscles already aching from the intense practice just moments ago. The sound of clinking weights fills the air as my teammates and I push ourselves to our limits, grinding through the best kind of pain. Practicing, lifting, and training until your body gives out is what champions are made of. This year, we have a real chance to take it all.

As I catch my breath between sets, flashes from last night's game flood my mind. We secured a hard-fought victory, and a win is a win, but mistakes were made. There's always something to learn, so I dissect each one in an effort to avoid repeating them.

"Heads-up," our equipment manager Eddy calls out.

I look up in time to catch the water bottle he tosses my way. I give him thanks with a nod of my head and take a long drink.

I readjust the weights on the leg press and begin my next set of reps. As much as I try to keep my head on my job, she keeps popping into my mind, and the mere seconds I saw her last night.

I noticed her talking to Beckett at the bar and wrapped up my conversation with a couple of fans. By the time I made it across the room to see her, she was hugging Beck goodbye. She congratulated me on a good game, gave me a half hug, and left. The interaction didn't last more than a minute.

It's unsettling, to say the least.

Beckett walks past, a towel on his shoulder. Sweat drips down his face.

"I think the point of the towel is to wipe the sweat off," I call out.

He looks at me, takes a second to register what I said, and then shakes his head with a smile. Grabbing the towel, he collects the massive amount of sweat on his skin. "Happy?"

"Better." I finish my last leg press, then slide out from the seat. "Hey, is everything okay with Iris? I only saw her briefly last night, but she rushed off quickly."

"Yeah, she's fine. She just needed some work advice. I have an appointment with Penny after this. Going to see about getting Iris a job here."

"Here? Doing what?"

"They posted an events coordinator job." He shrugs. "Thought it might be something she'd like."

"She's done with the whole lawyer thing?"

"For now. I'm not sure if she'll eventually go back to it but she needs a break."

Reaching back, I grab my towel from the weight bench and wipe my face. "Well, she'd be a good events coordinator. She's been planning parties since she was little."

"Right? I thought so, too. So we'll see what Penny has to say today."

Dr. Hoomeister, whom we affectionately call Hootie, wobbles through the room. He earned his nickname on appearance alone as he looks like a one-hundred-year-old white owl with his snow-colored hair, thick bottle-top glasses that make his eyes enormous, and his round face that carries a prominent pointy, beak-like nose. Of course, he assumes Hootie is a play on his last name. But the truth is, he made me believe in reincarnation. I'd be willing to bet all my money that the guy was an owl in his past life. It's the only explanation.

"Mr. Richards, Mr. Feldmore," Hootie chirps in a

high-pitched tone. Yes, the good doc speaks like a bird, too.

"What can we do for you, Hootie my man?" Beckett answers.

Dr. Hoomeister's thin lips form a smile. "Well, I was closing out some files, and I wanted to make sure your injuries have healed."

"Injuries?" Beck and I say in unison.

Hootie looks down at his clipboard, pushing his glasses up onto his nose. "Yes, Mr. Richards, I believe you had a concussion, and Mr. Feldmore a sprained ankle."

Beckett and I exchange glances, trying not to laugh. He speaks first, "My sprained ankle from October is just fine."

"So is my concussion," I add, though I don't know if it was a full-on concussion anyway. During a fight on the ice against Pittsburgh in mid-October, my helmet hit the ice, giving me a mild headache for a day. Once, when I was a teenager, my head hit the ice while skating with Beckett on the rink his dad had built for him in their backyard. That trauma left me dazed, puking, and with a killer headache for two weeks. That was a concussion.

The doctor peers up through his Coke bottle lenses. "So I can file this injury paperwork away?"

"Sure can. We're good, Doc." Beckett gives him a pat on the shoulder.

"Great." He nods. "Now, have you seen Mr. Dreven? I want to talk to him about that muscle he pulled."

I point toward the free weights. "Over there."

Hootie scurries away. Beckett and I look at each other and laugh under our breath.

"The Beast isn't going to be happy that Hootie is interrupting his workout to discuss a preseason groin pull. He has no patience for the doctor." Beck chuckles.

"Seriously, though. Wasn't that back in early September? It's January." I shake my head. "For as much money as this organization brings in, you'd think they could afford a better doctor. Hootie's awesome, but as a quirky next-door-neighbor type, not a doctor for professional athletes."

"Exactly. That's the job they should be posting."

The truth is, we don't go to Hootie for anything. We have two physical trainers on staff who are way more talented in the world of sports medicine than our elderly owl man.

"Though I've never seen him care about paper-work?" I raise a brow. "Maybe he's getting ready to retire?"

Beckett huffs out a laugh. "One could only hope."

Good luck with the new job today!

I stare at the text I sent Iris five hours ago. No response. Granted, she's working, and it's not a good look to whip out one's phone while in training. Yet the texts I sent this weekend asking if she had any plans or wanted to get together also went unanswered.

Barbados seems like such a distant memory. It's only been a few weeks, but it could've been a lifetime ago. The time we spent in Barbados was such a stark contrast to our interactions here that I sometimes wonder how it happened at all. I know I didn't dream up the whole thing, but damn, it sure feels as if I did.

I've barely seen Iris, and when I do, it's always short and cold greetings. The lingering feelings from Barbados are all but gone, at least for her. I'm not one to fool around with many women, but I thought there were emotions beyond the physical stuff we were doing. Perhaps, I'm being naive.

Face down, I swipe out of my text messages and click off my phone screen. When I look up, I abruptly stop so I don't run into her.

Iris looks up, startled. She was walking with her face down, staring at her phone, too.

"Texting someone?" I ask with a hopeful smile. Nice, Cade. Pathetic and needy.

She blinks, looking from me to her phone. She shakes her head. "Oh no. I'm reading the reviews for different food vendors."

"Oh, right. Already working hard. How do you like the new job?"

"Good. I mean, it's only been a few hours, but I'm already setting up something pretty big. It feels good to plan and be productive. You know how much I love making lists and getting stuff done."

"That I do." I allow my gaze to drift down her body. She looks beautiful in a pair of flowy black pants and a white blouse. Her hair cascades over her shoulders in waves, and her bright blue eyes pierce straight through to my heart like they always do. I want to reach out and hug her, but an invisible wedge between us stops me. "Do you want to celebrate with dinner this week? My treat. Anywhere you want to go."

She reaches her arm out and squeezes my wrist. "Thank you. That's so sweet, but I think I'll have to pass. I'll be working from morning to night this week to get this party planned in time. I'm not kidding when I say it's a lot to pull off in a week."

"Okay, no problem. Well, good luck. I'm sure it will be amazing."

She continues past me. "Thanks, and see you Friday."

"Friday?" I question, hopeful.

She looks back over her shoulder. "Yeah, at the party."

Right.

CHAPTER
NINETEEN

IRIS

Something resembling a smile crosses Penelope Stellars's face, a rarity. The woman is intimidating. She makes the grumpy old men I've worked with at the law office seem like a walk in the park. More than anything, she's hard to read. I've been training with her for a week, and I swear she's less than impressed with what I bring to the table. This might-be-a-grin that she's wearing now brings me so much pride I have to stop myself from jumping up in celebration.

I motion my hand around the room. "Everything look okay?"

She dips her chin and turns her assessing gaze toward me. "Everything looks great, Iris. There's a definite theme. It's welcoming and fun but classy. Just what I wanted. It will look great in pictures and videos." She slowly turns, scanning the space. "Just enough flair."

My heart beats triumphantly in my chest as genuine happiness warms my skin. "Thank you, Ms. Stellars."

"Please, I've told you to call me Penny."

"Thanks, Penny." I swallow hard. Her nickname rolling off my tongue makes me feel all sorts of weird. She carries too strong of a presence for a fun nickname. It'd be like walking into my advanced econ lecture with the toughest professor I've ever had, Dr. William Penfield, and addressing him as Billy. Immediate hives.

Pulling my clipboard from the bag, I say, "Should we go over the schedule one more time?"

"Yes, please," Penny answers.

I check the time. "Doors will open in an hour. Guests will receive their goody bag upon entry. The local TV stations and some hockey influencers will be here." I hand her a printed list of all the guests who will be sharing media from the event on the various socials. "Caterers are completing final touches in the kitchen as we speak. Waitstaff are getting dressed—"

She cuts me off. "In the…?"

"In the uniform you approved on Monday." She nods, and I continue. "The guys will arrive thirty minutes after the doors open. The schedule remains as discussed." I hand her a copy of the printed schedule of events we have fine-tuned all week. Her brown stare looks over the schedule, and her lips remain in a line. "Beckett assures me the guys will be on time."

Penny scoffs. "That would be a first."

"I think it's going to be a great event. We already have donations coming in, and I predict we will surpass our goal."

For decades, the team has had a nonprofit building company, Cranes Cares, to help people in need. Most projects include updating the homes for the elderly or people with special needs, such as adding handicap-accessible doors and wheelchair ramps. The company updates outdated electric boxes or other hazards and rebuilds leaky roofs and broken windows for those who can't afford to do it on their own.

Most people don't realize the hockey team runs the Cranes Cares building company. While the Cranes logo is a bird, they went with the machine version for the building company's logo.

One of the biggest tornadoes in northern Michigan wiped out a large portion of a small town made up of mostly farmers. It devastated this community. I secured my job by suggesting we plan a fundraiser to bring in enough money to rebuild many of the homes lost in that town. The guys had space in their schedule this weekend, so I made it happen in a week, a lofty goal for a seasoned event planner, let alone a first-time one. I knew I could do it, and I did. I've done everything in my power to make this night perfect.

"Great work, Iris." She hands me back the paper schedule. "Thank you."

"Of course," I say as Penny walks away.

The next hour flies by as I hurry around the hall, making sure everything is perfect. Guests begin arriving promptly at six, and the guys are all in attendance thirty minutes later as instructed. The food is delicious. The guys are friendly with the fans, as always. The two starting defensemen, Jaden and Max, film a TikTok with an influencer in the corner of the room while the other guys pose for photos, autograph various items, and talk to fans.

Everyone in the room seems to be having a great time.

I could get used to this.

Maybe this is the job for me. This week has been high energy, lots of organizing, and stressful in the best of ways. The result is beyond rewarding. Granted, I started my tenure as the Cranes event planner with a bang, organizing this charity event. I realize that most things I'll be working on won't be to this scale. I think Penny, and the boss that she is, was all about trial by fire. I'm sure she figured if I could survive this week, then I could hold my own in this organization. She has her hands full managing the guys, and I feel like she wanted to make sure the person who took this position wouldn't need their hand held.

"Amazing, Sis!" Beckett comes up to my side.

"Isn't it? I'm so happy with how everything turned out."

"Donations coming in?"

I look at Beck. "Yeah, they are. More than expected."

"Good, and if I'm not mistaken, you're pleased with yourself. Yeah?" He gives me a side smile.

I bite my bottom lip and grin. "Yeah, I am."

"So this position could be good for you?" He looks hopeful.

I shrug. "It's only been a week, but I think so. I mean, this is the most fun I've had in a job ever. I loved planning it all. I love working from the offices at the rink and seeing all the guys. It's just a good vibe."

"That's amazing. I'm happy you're happy."

"Thanks, Beck."

The night continues without incident, and we do, in fact, raise a record amount of donations. Every time Cade comes into view, some of the giddiness from the success of the evening is sucked from my body as I have to watch him with woman after woman, smiling and taking pictures. As freeing as Barbados was, I'm starting to wish it never happened in the first place.

I slam my fists against Beckett's apartment door in warning before using my spare key to let myself in. He comes stumbling out of his bedroom in his boxer shorts, bags under his eyes, and hair standing up straight on his head.

"What the fuck, Iris? Did someone die?"

"No." I close his apartment door behind me.

He runs his fingers through the disheveled mess atop his head. "Why are you here? I had another hour before I had to get up for practice." There's a whine in his voice, and I feel bad for stealing his sleep.

"I'm sorry, but I need to talk to you. I'm in crisis mode."

He exhales and plops down onto his couch. "When aren't you in crisis lately? You have to get your shit together, Sis." He yawns, pulling a throw blanket over his bare torso. "Can you make some coffee, please?"

"Sure." I nod and hurry to the kitchen. "And I'm trying to get my life together. That's why I'm here. I need someone to talk to."

"I'm not sure why you're choosing me. You know

Cade's always been better at advice. He'd be happy to help, especially during the early morning hours."

I quickly make two cups of coffee with Beckett's espresso maker. "I can't talk to Cade because it deals with him."

Beckett sits up, looking more awake with that last statement. He takes a cup of espresso from me. "Something's wrong with Cade?"

I sit in the oversized chair facing the couch. "I have something to tell you, something I've kept from you. I need you to hear me out before you comment and… remember that I'm an adult, not your baby sister."

"But you are my baby sister."

"No, I'm younger, sure. But I'm not a baby, Beck. I'm twenty-four years old, and this conversation can only be productive if you remember that fact."

He takes a sip of his coffee. "Okay, you're an adult. Go."

I hold up a finger. "Remember. Let me finish before you jump in. I need to get it all out before you start in with your dramatics."

"Got it." He raises his brows and pins me with a "get on with it" stare.

I blow out a breath and let the words flow like vomit. "So basically, I've been in love with Cade my whole life. We never did anything because of our friendship. Then the night of your graduation party, the two of us kissed. I thought it would finally lead to more, but instead, he told me that it couldn't happen again and walked away. His rejection crushed me. I was devastated and tried re-inventing myself. After that, I pulled away from you because being around Cade was too painful. Then the crap with Ben happened, and you convinced me to go to Barbados. I had a good time with Cade at Mom and Dad's anniversary party, so I figured it had been eight years, and I should just let Cade go and move on as friends. So that's what I tried to do. Yet something was different in Barbados. Cade seemed to feel everything I had always felt toward him, and we ended up fooling around. We didn't sleep together, but we definitely had... fun. We didn't agree to any sort of commitment, and I didn't know what to expect once we were back home. But seeing him flirting with girls every night, knowing that he's the 'heartbreaker' of the team, is really getting to me. I love my new job, but every time I see Cade with another woman, it's like salt in this wound that feels as if it has been opening and festering for years. I don't know how to get over him once and for all. And I need to find a way because if I don't, I won't be able to keep this job, and I really love it." My words come out in rapid succession, and with the last word, I pull much-needed air into my lungs and wait.

After a few beats, Beckett says, "I can talk now?"

I nod and then reconsider. "Wait, please don't be mad at me. For any of it."

"Well, first, I'm not mad or shocked or anything like that" —the corners of his lips tilt up—"because I already knew most of that."

"What? Cade told you?"

"No, he didn't." Beckett shakes his head with a chuckle. "You two obviously think I'm blind. You and Cade are my best friends, and I know you both inside and out. I knew you were into each other in high school. I knew something happened at the graduation party, and I definitely knew stuff was going on in Barbados."

"Why didn't you say anything?"

"Because it wasn't my place. Both of you know that you can talk to me about anything, and both of you chose to keep it between yourselves. I respected your right to privacy. I knew you'd come to me if you wanted to, but until then, I wasn't going to insert myself into a situation that neither of you wanted me in."

I drag my hands down my face. I did not expect to hear that from Beckett, and his admission makes me feel slightly idiotic that I believed he was clueless. "Wow."

"So you like Cade as in you want to be with him?" Beckett quirks a brow.

"I think so."

He shakes his head. "That's not enough. You have to know so. Cade has been in love with you for over a decade, and his feelings have never wavered. He's had enough pain in his life, so before you do anything, you have to be sure."

"If you haven't talked about this with him, what makes you so sure he's in love with me?"

"Because I know him. I see the way he looks at you. I see the way his face lights up when I talk about you. The guy has been infatuated with you from the moment you met."

"Then why is he so into other girls?" I cross my arms and lean back into the chair.

"I love you, Iris. But you need to learn to think things out rationally without the weight of your emotions clouding your view. Cade is not into other women. You say you've seen him with women this week? What have you seen him doing? Talking, laughing, taking pictures? That's part of the job. We're professional hockey players. We have fans. Of course he's going to talk to them. Have you ever known Cade to be rude to anyone? He's literally the nicest, most sincere guy in the world. Have you seen him kiss a girl?" He presses his forefinger of one hand to the forefinger of his other as he ticks off each question. "Leave with a girl? Do anything with a girl that he would do with a guy fan? No, you haven't."

"Okay, maybe not this week, but I'm sure in the past. He has a nickname for a reason, Beck. I don't want to set myself up for heartbreak by dating the team's heartbreaker."

Beckett lets his head fall back and laughs. Shaking his head, he looks at me. "Oh, Iris…" He sighs. "He got the nickname because he breaks hearts by not giving girls a chance in the first place. He's one of the most eligible bachelors on the team, and he won't give even the hottest woman his time. He'll chat with them, laugh with them, and have a genuine conversation, but he doesn't let it go past that. He doesn't take women back to his room. He doesn't do random hookups. The guy is basically a saint, and the fact that you can't see that makes me question your higher-level thinking skills."

"Well, how was I supposed to know that?" I throw my arms up in the air.

"By opening your eyes." Beckett scoffs. "As I said, I love you… but you're so focused on your own feelings you don't truly see him."

"If you knew all this, why didn't you say something!" I shriek.

"As I said, you never asked."

"You could've saved me a lot of grief," I snap.

"I know you think I'm just a beautiful idiot." He puckers his lips, and I can't help but laugh. "But I see people, and while I saw everything that was going on, I also knew that if you two were going to work, you both had to deal with your own issues first, which takes time. It's an individual thing, Iris. It didn't work at my graduation because you two weren't ready. I'm not sure that you're ready now." He shrugs.

"I want to be ready." I swallow the emotion in my throat.

"Do you love him?"

Thinking for a moment, I answer, "I think so, yeah. What should I do?"

"Well, first, you need to talk to Cade. Be open and honest. Have a discussion like two grown adults. Don't resort to running or hiding your emotions. Let it all out. And listen."

I nod. "I can do that."

"Iris," he says my name on an exhale.

"Yeah?"

"I'm serious. Listen to Cade. The decisions he's made have little to do with you and everything to do with him. He walked away from you at that graduation party for a reason. If you love him, you have to be there for him too. He deserves a partner who will lift him up and make his life better. I know he'd do that for anyone he loves, and I just want to make sure that the woman lucky enough to capture Cade Richards's heart knows what she's got and loves him the way he's worthy of."

I take in my brother now. The words coming from his mouth clash with what I see when I look at him. He's right. I've always thought of him as a handsome, fun-loving, womanizing jokester. Now, I'm realizing maybe I don't know him as well as I think I do. Certainly not as well as he knows me.

Some of his words sting, but I can't deny he's right. I've never taken the time to look past my pain and into Cade's. He was supposed to be my best friend, and because I was hurt, I cut him off—for years. I've been selfish, but in my defense, I was lost, drowning in self-doubt. It's easy to only think about oneself when you're struggling to keep your head above water. Survival has the canny ability to turn anyone into an egotistical jerk.

I'm done.

Life has to be about more than surviving. I'm ready to be brave enough to live.

CHAPTER
TWENTY

CADE

I down a glass of water and set the cup in the sink before I continue to pace through my condo. Glancing at my phone, I take note that it's been twenty-two minutes since Iris texted. A vast two-minute difference since I last checked. I don't know why I'm so uneasy about this whole thing. At this point, it will be what it will be. There's no use getting all worked up over it. Yet when the girl of your dreams texts *Can I come over? We need to talk.* It's either going to be an amazing night or an incredibly shitty one.

Finally, there's a knock on the door. I hurry across the room, take a deep breath, and open the door.

All sense of worry leaves my body as her presence calms me. She wears a pair of black leggings, a baggy sweatshirt, no makeup, and her hair up in a messy bun. She's gorgeous.

She smiles and lifts the Tupperware container in her hands. "I brought cookies. Apparently, they're only bronze medal worthy." She rolls her eyes with a huff. "But they're still damn delicious."

Opening the door wide, I stand to the side and motion her in. She hands me the container of cookies, and it's warm on the bottom. "I told ya, they're five stars to me. They're still warm."

"Yeah, I just took them out of the oven." She toes off her boots onto the rug, and I close the door behind her. "I always think chocolate chip cookies are better when they're still warm, you know? Do you have any milk?" She makes her way into the kitchen and opens the refrigerator door.

She looks over her shoulder, and an accusatory stare finds me.

I laugh. "I'm rarely here. It's really not worth keeping a stocked fridge."

"Cade, this is sad. Like really sad. You don't even have the basics." She opens the produce drawer, which is filled with all my fast food sauce packets—soy sauce, spicy mustard, ketchup, ranch, Chick-fil-A sauce, and Taco Bell Fire sauce. "First of all, these don't need to be refrigerated. And then let's see." She closes the sauce drawer and looks at the fridge door, where half-empty bottles of ranch, sriracha, and honey mustard sit. "You have three most likely expired condiments and"—with a sigh, she grabs the apple on the top shelf—"one questionable apple. This is seriously concerning, Cade."

I hold up my hands. "In my defense, I just threw out a bunch of to-go boxes of food. There was more stuff in there. As I said, I'm never here. It's easier to get takeout."

"But what about breakfast and snacks and stuff?" She closes the refrigerator door and turns to face me.

"Oh, I got that covered." I open the walk-in pantry door next to the refrigerator to reveal shelves of different flavors and brands of protein shakes.

She chuckles. "Well, glad you're getting your protein, but still. Very pathetic, Cade. What about wine? Do you possess any of that?"

I open the cupboard above the sink and pull out a bottle of red wine with a fancy label containing green foil holly leaves and gold embossed writing that says, "We wish you a Feldmore Christmas."

"Tada," I state.

"The bottle of wine handed out at my parents' Christmas party three years ago?" Her chest heaves with laughter. With a shake of her head, she takes the bottle from me. "Well, at least I know it's good wine. Cookies and red wine aren't my favorite, but it will have to do."

We fill two wineglasses and take them with the container of cookies and a couple of plates to the living room.

Sitting on the sofa, I take a sip of wine. "I'm overdue for a shopping trip. My kitchen isn't always so barren." Not that she would know because this is the first time she's been to my condo.

"Uh-huh." She purses her lips and looks around the living room. "There aren't any pictures on the walls or anything. How long have you lived here?"

"A couple of years."

"A couple of years?" she shrieks. "Cade, it looks like you just moved in. You haven't personalized your space at all." Her face falls in disgust.

I shrug with a chuckle. "What can I say? I'm gone a lot. I guess I didn't see the point in decorating a place I basically use for sleep."

"Well." She releases a sigh. "I'll help you fix it." She picks at the cookie between her fingers, then sets it on her plate. "I think we're like eight years overdue for a serious talk."

Twisting to face her, I swallow. "Okay."

She blows out a breath. "I just feel like everything is messed up. I was so mad at you for so long, and then Barbados happened, and it was different. You know? But then we get back here to normal life, and I could no longer ignore all the things I could conveniently forget while I was in Barbados."

"Why were you mad at me for so long?"

Her eyes go wide. "Are you serious? I'm not saying that in a mean way, but like, you really don't know?"

"No. I don't know."

She shakes her head and presses her fingers to her temples. "Okay, first. Let's just make sure we're on the same page. You liked me in high school and knew I liked you too. Right?"

"Yeah."

"Okay, and then Barbados…that was all real attraction. Right?"

"Of course. I'm confused. Do you think I was faking any of that?" I lean forward, wanting to be closer to her.

"No." She blows out a breath. "I just wanted to make sure we're on the same page before launching into everything that hurt me. I would feel like an idiot if I had imagined any of it. Let's just start at the graduation party. I…" She rubs her palms across her thighs and swallows. "I don't think you realize how much your dismissal that night changed the trajectory of my life. I mean, I thought you loved me as much as I loved you, and when you walked away, it crushed me. I questioned who I was. I'm being completely honest when I say that your rejection broke my heart, Cade.

Completely shattered it. I still don't understand why you rejected me." Her voice cracks, and she drops her eyes to her lap. A tsunami of guilt crashes over me.

"I'm so sorry, Iris." I reach for her hand, but she pulls it away. I sigh. "Listen... I did love you then. I loved you so much, but..."

She raises her face, her blue eyes filled with unshed tears.

"I wasn't good enough for you." The truth I've been holding in escapes.

"What do you even mean? Of course you were."

I shake my head. "I wasn't. At least in my head, I wasn't. I realize now, after many years of self-reflection and the maturity to process it all that my insecurities were in my head. At the time, though, they were very real. I never felt good enough for you, Iris. For my whole life, I felt like an afterthought, an impostor. Here I was, the foster kid, hanging out with the Feldmore kids. It didn't seem real. For years, I kept thinking the rug would be pulled out from under me, and I'd discover that it was all just a prank or that you two saw me as some charity case. I know it sounds stupid now. But I can't describe what a decade of rejection does to the fabric of oneself. At my core, I felt unlovable."

"But you knew I loved you."

I bite the corner of my lip and shrug, lifting my gaze to meet hers. "I knew you thought you did but feared you'd see through me and realize I wasn't enough. In a life full of so much rejection, I couldn't bear being rejected by you, so I ended it before it had the chance to begin. I walked away from you, vowing that I'd become enough. I thought if I could make something of myself and become truly successful, I might be worthy of you."

"It's been eight years, Cade." A tear falls down her cheek.

"I know. I was so focused on making it and becoming successful so I could give you the life you deserved. But we grew apart, and you moved on. You had your job and your boyfriend. There was no place for me anymore, so I kept my distance. You seemed happy, and I wouldn't ruin that for you. It killed me not to be able to talk to or touch or love you the way I wanted, but I'd made my choice and lost you. As long as you were happy, I'd have to live with that. Things changed when I saw you at your parents' anniversary party and realized you weren't happy."

"So what? You thought I wouldn't love you until you were making millions?" Her voice raises an octave.

"It sounds ridiculous, I know, but kind of... yeah."

She wraps her arms around her chest and rocks back. "That's so messed up, Cade."

"Believe me, I know."

"Just so you know, I wasn't happy. I was miserable.

I created this version of myself that could live without you, and I hated her."

"I wish it could've been different, Iris. The fact is, I couldn't have been the man that you deserved because I didn't love myself. I was hurting, and I refused to hurt you in the process. I realize that my actions did exactly that, but you have to know that I walked away because I loved you."

She stands with a huff. "This is so stupid. So much heartache. So much wasted time. For nothing." Hands on her hips, she shifts back and forth on her feet.

I rise and take a step toward her. "I know, and I'm sorry."

She throws her hands up. "The slightest bit of communication could've saved us so much heartache."

Placing my hands on her arms, I say, "We were young, just teens. I don't think either of us handled it well, but we coped with the skills we had at the time. It's easy to look back and think things could've been different if we had done this or that. I think we needed the past eight years to find ourselves so we could be good for each other."

"So you want to be together now?" She lifts her face to meet my stare.

"Yeah, I do." I take her chin between my thumb and forefinger and bring her face toward mine. Our lips meet, and I'm overcome with emotion. We shared many kisses in Barbados, but this is the first real kiss we've had at home where I don't want to run. I want to stay with her forever.

She pulls away and lifts her hand to my cheek. "Now I'm the one with insecurities."

"What do you mean?" I circle my hands around her hips and pull her closer to me, wanting to feel the warmth of her body.

"I'm afraid." She sighs. "It's different now. Back then, it was you and me... and Beck"—she grins— "against the world. Now you have women falling at your feet, wanting to be with you everywhere you go. And I know Barbados was fun, but something held you back. You weren't all in."

"Of course I was all in."

"No, you weren't. You only let me please you once, and you refused to sleep with me. I'm still recovering from your rejection eight years ago. I can't let myself fall again only for you to crush me again."

I release a long breath and take her face in my hands. Bringing my lips to her forehead, I press them against her skin. "Oh, Rosie." A grin finds my lips. "You have no idea." I inch my face back and hold her stare. "I don't care about any woman but you. You have nothing to worry about. My mind, body, and soul have a singular focus, and it's you. I didn't sleep with you in Barbados because when I do, it won't be a vacation fling. It's going to be forever."

"Really?" Emotion lodges in her throat, and she swallows.

"Yeah. I love you, Iris. I've waited my whole life to be with you. Believe me, not sleeping with you in Barbados took all my willpower, but I had to make sure you were mine. I've been saving my first time for you. It's always only ever been you."

She blinks. "Wait? You've never slept with anyone?"

I shake my head. "I believe we get one fucking love in this lifetime, and you're mine."

CHAPTER
TWENTY-ONE

IRIS

C ade, Mr. Heartbreaker himself, is a virgin? It doesn't seem real. He's had women throwing themselves at him for years, and he's never given in to temptation? How is that possible?

"Are you serious? You've never messed around with anyone?"

"I've messed around with girls, sure, but nothing serious. And it's never gone all the way. I wouldn't let it." He takes my hands in his, rubbing his thumb against my skin.

"But I was dating someone. I slept with him and others before him. How could you wait for me when I was taken? I didn't wait for you."

His mouth turns up into a grin, his expression

warm and nonjudgmental. "I never expected you to. I get that it sounds weird, but I knew deep in my heart that you were the one for me. I've never wanted to be with other women. I've only ever wanted you. For me, sleeping around would've never filled the hole in my life that only you can fill. I don't blame you for exploring relationships with others. That was part of your journey—the one that led you here. But my journey was working on myself and waiting for you."

"I don't even know what to say." I bring my palm to Cade's face, cupping his cheek. "This is a lot." I run my thumb across his stubble.

"What do you want, Rosie?" He moves his face to the side and kisses my fingers.

Years of emotion, desire, and affection rise to the surface. I can hardly process everything we've discussed. It's a mess to unpack. There's an element of regret filling my chest. I've spent so much time being angry, hating him, and doubting myself. For what? He's loved me all along.

It's sad, really. So much wasted time.

A tear slips from my eye, and I drop my hand.

Cade tucks an errant strand of hair that's slipped from my bun behind my ear. "Do you want to be together, Iris? No more games, regrets, or palm tree avoidance. Just you and me, all in. Committed to one another. It will be real, raw, and vulnerable but incredible. I'm ready if you are."

Another tear falls and then another. My heart is so full, and I'm overwhelmed with gratitude. Maybe Cade is right, and we wouldn't have worked back then. Perhaps we had to go through the struggles of the past eight years to be in a place where we could have a lasting relationship. Though, I'm not that far removed from a total life meltdown—

heck, I might very well still be in the midst of my crisis—everything about committing to Cade feels right.

I nod, and a grin finds Cade's face. "I'm going to need to hear the words, babe."

Pulling in a breath, I clear my throat. "I'm yours, Dummy. I've always been yours."

His lips find mine, and I kiss him with everything I have. Cade is an incredible kisser and can do magical things with his tongue. But this kiss is better than any other because for the first time ever, it's void of uncertainty. It's pure love.

"Do you want to go to bed?" I say against his lips, my voice hoarse with need. I've never desired anything as much as I want Cade right now.

"Fuck yes," he growls. Picking me up from the ground, I wrap my legs around his waist. He leads us to his bedroom, kissing me the whole way.

Once in his bedroom, we make quick work of removing our clothes. I stand naked before Cade. His hazel stare scans my body from my toes to my face, heating my skin.

He cups the back of my neck and pulls me in for another kiss. "I don't have condoms," he says.

"We don't need them."

He inches his face away and lifts a brow. "I'm on birth control, and I got tested for everything after Ben. I'm clean, but we can wait for another time."

"I don't want to wait." He shakes his head. "That's good enough for me." He trails kisses down my neck and to my collarbone. "It will be nice to have nothing between us, anyway."

"Are you nervous?" I scratch my nails against the skin of his back.

"Yeah, a little." He forces a laugh. "It's stupid, I know."

I cradle his face, forcing him to look me in the eye. "It's not stupid at all. If you want to stop at any time, just say the word."

"No." His eyes widen. "I definitely don't want to stop. I'm just nervous I won't live up to..." His voice trails off.

I kiss him. "I have no worries. You're already the master of foreplay. You're amazing at everything you set your mind to, so I know this will be no different."

We crawl up onto Cade's bed, and his mouth deliciously explores my body. The guy is about to have sex for the first time, and his priority is making sure I'm taken care of. The anticipation builds, and it's almost too much. Cade has positioned his face between my legs. I thread my fingers through his hair as he licks until I squirm.

I didn't know if I'd get this again after Barbados, and I'm so relieved I do. "Cade," I pant, grabbing at his shoulder. "I want to come together."

His mouth moves away, and he trails kisses up my body, stopping to give each nipple extra attention. He continues upward until I'm caged between his arms that press against the mattress on either side of my face. He brings his mouth to mine and kisses me. His lips are so soft and full against mine. I thread my fingers through the hair at the nape of his neck and kiss him with everything I have. I could kiss him forever.

"I can't believe this is happening," he whispers against my lips.

Moving his hips, he positions his length at my entrance. I open my legs wider, desperate for him to be inside me. "Say you're really mine."

"I'm yours, Cade. Only yours. Claim me." I move my hips forward, inching the tip of his dick inside me.

His breath is ragged. He holds my stare, his mouth falling open as he pushes inside.

"Oh fuck." His eyes roll back as he moves. His pace increases. I circle my legs around him, and he groans as he goes deeper. I move my hips, meeting him thrust for thrust, wanting him harder and faster. A thin sheen of sweat appears against his skin as I dig my fingers into his back.

"Cade." His name comes out on an exhale as the orgasm in my body builds.

"You feel so good." His face falls to mine, and his tongue enters my mouth, mirroring the actions of our bodies below.

"Are you close? I want to come together." My whole body vibrates, waiting to fall.

"Uhh...yeah..." he grunts and pounds into me, hitting my back wall. Stars erupt beneath my eyelids as my orgasm hits hard and fast.

I cry out as I crash into oblivion.

"Fuck...uhhh," Cade groans as he comes inside me, our bodies shuddering together in sheer bliss.

I knew it would be good, and it was perfect. Everything about being with Cade feels right and so incredible.

He lays atop me, breathing heavy, his chest rising and falling with each audible breath. He plants a quick kiss on my lips and rolls off me, falling to the bed. He presses his hand to his chest, above his heart as his breaths calm. "That was"—he swallows—"amazing."

I roll to my side and prop my head up. "Was it everything you wanted it to be?"

He turns to face me and tucks a strand of hair behind my ear. His answer is thick with emotion. "So much more."

A burst of laughter bubbles up in my throat, and I cover my mouth.

"What is it?" he asks.

I shake my head. "I just can't believe I slept with Cade Richards," I squeal, causing him to chuckle.

"I can't believe I slept with Iris Feldmore."

"We've waited a long time for this." I trace his collarbone with my finger.

"Yeah, we have. There were times when I never thought it would happen," he admits.

My fingers continue to move across his chest, tracing the lines of his muscles. It's still surreal touching Cade so freely like this. My sixteen-year-old self would've combusted in hormonal ecstasy. "How long were you going to wait for me? I dated Ben for a year. I'm surprised you waited. That's a long time."

"I don't know." He drags his thumb over my lips, looking at me with such reverence. "I just knew I wasn't ready to let the dream of you go just yet. Deep down, I felt we were inevitable. With us, it was always the right person, wrong time. Our timelines needed to sync, and they did."

We're quiet for a moment, exploring one another's body and taking it all in.

I'm no life expert, but I'd venture to say that finally getting the person I've always wanted and connecting through mind-blowing sex is the ideal cure for a quarter-life crisis. I feel whole and happier than I've been in years.

"Iris?"

"Yeah."

"Can we do that all again?"

I laugh, my body already humming in anticipation. "God, yes."

The second my response leaves my mouth, Cade crashes his lips to mine.

CHAPTER
TWENTY-TWO

CADE

R eaching over to my nightstand, I turn off the alarm on my phone that is set to go off in two minutes, not wanting it to wake Iris. Her bare back rises and falls in slumber, and it takes everything in me not to kiss every inch of it. I already miss her, and I haven't left yet.

We've spent every possible minute together this past week that we could. I love that I can see her at work. Just knowing she's up in the offices, a flight of stairs away from where I practice on the rink, makes me happy. She cheers me on from the stands at every home game and comes home to my bed every night.

The transition to dating has been seamless. Since our relationship is rooted in friendship, everything has progressed naturally and has felt effortless. It turns out, my feelings for Iris weren't as remotely secret as I thought they were. Apparently, Beckett knew we'd get together before we even did.

I've had more sex in this past week than I thought was humanly possible, and I'm aching for more. I now completely understand Beckett's whore era. Hand jobs and BJs are good and all, but they don't compare to the real deal. Maybe it's this amazing with everyone, or perhaps it's just because it's Iris and me, but I had no idea how incredible sex would be. Now that I've slept with Iris, it's all I want to do.

With as little sound as possible, I roll out of bed and head to the shower. My muscles ache from a combination of exhaustion and exertion. As incredible as this week has been, this new normal is taking its toll. It's clear I need more sleep, and eventually, I'll get it. Right now, my relationship with Iris is too new. I don't want to miss a second with her.

With a yawn, I close the bathroom door behind me and turn on the shower. Half asleep, I brush my teeth while the shower heats, causing the mirrors to fog. I step into the shower with an exhale. Standing beneath the hot water, I allow the spray to soothe my muscles and wake my senses.

The glass door moves, and I look to see Iris stepping in.

"You left me." She splays her hands across my chest.

I kiss her forehead. "I was trying to let you sleep. You don't have to get up for a couple of hours."

Her hands travel from my chest and down my abs. "I hate not seeing you before you leave." She stands on her toes and kisses me.

I groan in her mouth as her hand takes hold of my already hard and ready shaft. "I hate not seeing you, too. But I wanted you to get your sleep," I say through a moan as she moves her hand.

"Sleep is overrated," she says against my wet skin as she kisses down my neck and over my pec.

My head falls back as the pace of her hand increases, and I groan. I take hold of her arms and spin her around so she's facing away and pull her back to my front. She bends her head to the side, allowing me access. I suck on the delicate skin at the base of her neck and press my palms down the front of her body, over her breasts, abdomen, and onto her thighs.

"Leg," I utter as my hand slides between her thighs. She raises one leg and rests it on the edge of the tub, allowing me access. I slide two fingers into her opening, and she whimpers, leaning her head back against my shoulders. Working my fingers in and out, I slide them over her sensitive bundle of nerves and back into her entrance, repeating the motion until she's moaning, clawing at my arm, and thrusting her hips into my hand.

She audibly protests when I pull my fingers away. I twist her body and press her against the tiled wall. Hiking up one of her legs with my arm, I use my other to position myself between her legs. I hold her stare with mine wanting to see her face as I enter. Her mouth falls open in a sigh, and her eyes roll back as I push myself deep inside her.

"Does that feel good?"

She grips my hips. "So good."

Leaning my forehead against hers, I move inside her as my senses prepare for release. Pleasure radiates through every inch of my body. I'm convinced it can't feel this good for everyone. Iris's body was made for me, and mine for her. We're a perfect pair.

Body pressed against hers, I spread my free hand against the tile above her head. "I'll never get enough of you," I groan.

"I'm counting on it." Her voice trembles as her body shakes. "Cade," she cries out.

The sound of her release fuels my own, and we fall into ecstasy together.

I pull out of her and drop her leg. Cradling her face, I kiss her, moving my tongue against hers. "I love you." I pull my face away.

"I love you."

I press another kiss to her forehead and grab the bottle of body wash. She takes the loofah and holds it out for me. I squeeze the body wash onto it and steal it from her grasp.

"Hey, I want to wash you," she protests.

"No way. We both know where that will lead, and I can't be late again." I scrub the loofah against my body.

She runs her hands along my shoulders. "What's ten minutes?"

"To Coach Albright? A lot. As much as I want you... again, I'm not going to be on the end of his wrath today. Today is not the day to be late with our game in Montreal tomorrow." I use the loofah to move her hands from my body.

"Rude." She crosses her arms and narrows her stare.

I quickly rinse the soap from my body and plant a chaste kiss against Iris's lips. "Enjoy the rest of your shower. I'll see you in a couple of hours."

"Okay." She squeezes my hand, and I step out.

Getting to practice on time was the right call. Sweat drips down my face as I finish drills, which ran twice as long as normal. Coach is always strung up tight before we face Montreal. It's personal with him. Apparently, he played against their coach back in the day, and while the rivalry was strong, it wasn't friendly. Winning tomorrow means more to Coach than he'll admit.

"Quick drink and then on the ice! You know the drill," Coach bellows.

I suppress an exhausted groan, and instead yell, "Yes, Coach!"

Beckett tips his head back and squeezes water from the water bottle into his mouth. "I hate Montreal week."

"Same." I wipe my face with a towel and reposition my helmet before stepping back on the ice.

We scrimmage, and Coach plays around with different combinations of players on the ice. He does this every once in a while, having a need to triple-check the ability of varying player lineups. It's exhausting to give a hundred percent again and again as Coach demands more run-throughs. At the same time, it's the best. The endorphin release and high that courses through me after demanding so much of my body is unmatched, or prior to Iris it was anyway. Now, it's a close second.

After hours of practice, Coach calls out the starting lineup with Dreven as goalie, Beckett and me as the right and left wings, Bash as the center, and Jaden and

Max as the two defensemen—which is the lineup we've started with all season. We all knew the result would be the same, but if it gives Coach peace of mind, then so be it.

"Go home and rest up. Eat well and get a good night's sleep tonight. If anyone shows up for the flight tomorrow tired or hungover, you can find a new fucking job!" Coach dismisses us.

"Yes, Coach!" the team yells in unison.

Coach Albright hurries out of the arena.

Max skates up beside me. "The guy is going to give himself an aneurysm. He really needs to take up yoga or something, anything that will help him with that stress."

I scoff. "Agreed."

"You know sex is the best stress relief there is," Jaden adds. "Coach needs to get laid."

"His wife left him last year." I take a seat on the bench and untie my skates.

Beckett pulls off his helmet and huffs with raised eyebrows. "I wonder why."

"What are you guys thinking about Montreal tomorrow? They have a good record this year." I cringe, thinking of our loss to them at the beginning of the season.

"Yeah, and their new goalie is fire," Jaden states

before calling over his shoulder. "Though he has nothing on the Beast, Gunner Dreven, himself!"

Dreven grunts and heads toward the locker room.

Beckett follows Dreven. "We can do it. We're having an incredible season, too. They don't have anything we don't. We need to win this one for Coach. You know the guy's not getting laid, so giving him a win against his rival is the least we can do."

The team files into the locker room and into the showers. There's less shit talk and joking around than normal. I imagine everyone feels as utterly exhausted as I do. The practice was brutal. After the shower, I dry off and throw on some sweats.

Beckett and I head out together. Before stepping out of the locker room, Beckett shouts, "Remember what Coach said, good food, sleep, and sex! See you tomorrow, boys!"

"He didn't say anything about sex." I chuckle, tossing my duffel over my shoulder.

"It was implied." He eyes me. "And just because you're finally getting some doesn't mean I want to hear about it. I'm cool with you and Iris and all, but I don't need details. She's still my sister."

"Uh, yeah... wasn't planning on sharing any of that with you. I've never been a kiss-and-tell type of guy. You know that. Hell knows, I'm not going to start over-sharing now that I'm with your sister."

"Just making sure."

"Noted." I shake my head as we head through the door to the parking structure. "But while we're on the subject, feel free to keep all your sex details to yourself, too. I've never really cared to hear about it, and that hasn't changed."

We approach our vehicles. "Sorry, bud." He shrugs. "I'm an oversharer, and you're my best friend, so you will hear all about my night tomorrow."

"Maybe I'll get lucky, and you'll strike out tonight."

Beckett laughs. "Not a chance, my guy. See you tomorrow."

CHAPTER
TWENTY-THREE

IRIS

Penelope Stellars cradles her Trenta pumpkin spiced latte between her two hands and sips it so slowly it's almost arousing. Her eyelids, with perfectly winged black liner, are closed as she drinks the coffee in slow swallows. I literally can't pull my eyes away. I don't think I've ever seen anyone enjoy a coffee drink as much as Penny loves her PSLs.

"I love you, Iris Feldmore." She sighs, pulling the cup from her red lips.

Penny is an enigma that I can't quite figure out. She's always dressed to impress with expertly applied makeup and her long red hair twisted in an updo. She's a hard worker and almost militant in how she handles the team's PR. Some days, I'm scared to death of her and completely intimidated, and other times—like now—she seems so vulnerable. She holds the coffee cup like a lifeline. It's definitely the best twenty dollars I've spent in a while.

Cade told me about Penny and her affinity toward pumpkin-spiced lattes. Apparently, the woman is obsessed with pumpkins, autumn, and all things fall-related, but she loves pumpkin-flavored coffee drinks the most. As it happens, I have a PSL connection with my friend Megan. I met Megan while attending undergrad at the University of Michigan. She actually dropped out of law school and works at the Ann Arbor campus Starbucks. Conveniently, she's dating the store manager, Henry, and convinced him to let her hoard a couple of bags of the PSL mix. I think she held on to the mix initially because she loved PSLs and the coffee shop only carries them late August through November. But now she's turned her secret PSL mix into a side hustle, selling the pumpkin-flavored drink to her friends in the offseason for a hefty markup.

This is the third cup I've brought Penny, and I'm pretty sure we're now best friends.

"I don't know how you do it, but I can't tell you how much joy this brings me. As popular as this drink is, I don't see why they can't carry it all year. I've tried duplicating it at home, but my attempts are not good."

Penny turns her brown-eyed stare my way. The airplane hits some turbulence, and we bounce in our seats. "Montreal is a bitch of a game, especially when it's away. Any games with big rivalries and high stakes wind the guys up." She sighs. "And when they're wound tight, they like to let loose, and we all know what a PR nightmare they can be after some drinks, especially in a crowd of their rival's fans." She sighs. "I never thought I would use my master's degree to be a glorified babysitter for grown-ass men."

"Do you like your job?" The question is hesitant. Had I not supplied Penny with her favorite thing in the world, I wouldn't have the balls to ask it. "With your qualifications, you could work anywhere."

She blinks, her face still. Her eyes stare off as she formulates an answer. She shrugs with a roll of her eyes. "You know what? I do. Not sure why, and God knows I complain about it... a lot. But I secretly love it."

"Really?" I grin. "I was not expecting that answer."

She quirks a brow. "Well, don't tell anyone. Having the whole team think I hate my job and life has its perks." She holds her cup of coffee. "I get all sorts of presents. Case in point. Though." She points a finger my way. "I'd appreciate if my pumpkin-flavored caffeinated gifts continue."

I chuckle. "Of course, I'll keep 'em coming as long

as I can. My friend said she's starting to run low on the mix."

"Ugh," Penny says dramatically. "Why is the winter so gosh darn long? It's never-ending torture." She leans her head back against the airplane seat.

"I know, right?"

The sound of the guys' laughter catches my attention, and I look forward to see a group of them, Cade included, talking adamantly about something.

I would've loved to sit next to Cade on the plane, but I guess the guys have their spots. They sit in the same seats on the way to and from every game for good luck, a team superstition.

Penny must notice my line of sight. "Cade's a good guy. One of the best, actually."

"Yeah, he is. I got lucky."

Looking away from the guys, I turn back toward Penny. Feeling brave, I lower my voice and ask, "Have you dated any of the guys on the team?"

Her eyes widen. "God, no. Never."

"Really?" I chuckle. "You're serious about that."

"Definitely. You see, my job is to be the bad guy. I need the guys to respect me, and better yet... fear me, so they'll listen. A relationship would never work." She quickly adds, "Not that there is anyone I'd want to date anyway."

She added that last part a little too quickly. I can't say I agree with her. The team consists of grown-ass men who know how to respect a woman. Penny has carved out this version of herself that she thinks works best for her role, but I'd be willing to bet the guys would respect a more cheerful version of Penny just as much. But I don't tell her that.

"Go! Go! Gooo!" I shriek at the top of my lungs. My arms flail in the air as I jump up and down in front of my seat. The arena is deafeningly loud as the screams of the Montreal fans boom around me. It's been a long game full of one back and forth and close call after the next. The teams are tied one to one with a minute left in the third period.

Cade intercepted the puck on a Montreal pass near our net and rushes down the ice toward Montreal's goal. He's so fast on the ice as he breaks away from the others. My heart beats rapidly in my chest, and my throat hurts from screaming, but I don't stop. We have to get this. "Go!" The roar around me all but mutes my scream, but this game makes me so anxious that I have to yell to release the tension in my body.

Even Penelope, in her patent-leather Louis Vuitton pumps, bounces beside me, arms raised as she urges Cade on.

Montreal's defenders charge Cade as he closes in on the goal, but he slaps the puck over to Beckett before they reach him. In a fast break that I would've missed if I'd blinked, Beckett strikes the puck, and it goes flying toward Montreal's goal. I hold my hands to my mouth. The goalie reaches out for the puck, but it slides through the small space between the goalie's glove and the edge of the net.

"Goal for the Cranes!" the announcer yells.

Penny and I scream and hug one another, jumping up and down.

The forty-five seconds left in the game tick by, and we pull out a two-to-one win. Our fans are in the minority in this stadium, but they're loud as they cheer on the guys.

Our guys pump their fists in the air and hug one another in celebration. Cade and Bash pick up Beckett and skate him back and forth as he yells out, a huge smile on his face. My vision blurs with happy tears threatening to spill over. This was the best game I've ever been to.

I can't believe I let so many years pass without fully immersing myself into this sport that my brother loves so much. I've attended many games over the years and have always been happy when the guys won but couldn't fully let my emotions fly because I was wrung too tight, holding on to my hurt over Cade. Nothing is better than experiencing a hockey game where Cade, Beckett, and the rest of the team that I've grown to love play with their entire hearts and win. This game is thrilling.

"Come on! Let's go greet the guys before they head to the locker room," I say to Penny.

We weave through the crowd of disappointed Montreal fans and head down to the entrance of the visiting team's locker room. I hold out my hand, giving the guys high fives as they enter the locker room. When Beckett reaches me, he pulls me into a hug and gives me a spin.

"Congrats on the winning goal, Beck. You played so well tonight." I squeeze him tight.

He sets me down. "Thanks, Sis! That was a hell of a game." He moves on to Penny and lifts her into a hug despite her shrill protest.

Cade steps toward me, and I throw my arms around him, pressing my mouth to his. "I'm so proud of you. Amazing game!" Cade scored the first goal and gave Beckett the assist for the second. He truly is so talented.

"Thank you." He smiles wide. "It felt incredible. Such a rush." He kisses me again. "Made even better because you're here. I'm going to shower so we can start celebrating." His lips find mine once more, and he slaps my ass as he passes.

I'm so grateful the Cranes organization flew me here to watch the team play. There's a short meet and greet with some fans and press right after this, but it's all set up. There's no reason I have to be here as far as my employers are concerned , but they sent me anyway. I've only been working with the team for a couple of weeks, yet I already feel like part of the Cranes family. It's an incredible family to be a part of.

Scrolling through my phone, I double-check the information for the press conference. "The guys need to head to room C3 when they finish changing," I tell Penny.

"Okay." She nods.

After a few minutes, the guys start exiting the locker room with smiles on their faces. Penny leads a group to the conference room.

Coach Albright exits wearing an uncharacteristic grin. "Great game, Coach."

"Thank you, Ms. Feldmore," he says. I'm taken aback by the fact that he knows who I am. I haven't had more than a couple of seconds of interaction with the man. Second, I never realized how alarmingly attractive he is for a middle-aged man. I suppose a smile goes a long way to boost a person's physical appeal.

Cade and Beck exit, bags over their shoulders. They face one another, talking animatedly. I love seeing their connection. Childhood friends often grow apart as they get older, and I'm so happy that Cade and Beckett have only grown closer.

They each step to the side when they spot me, allowing me space between them.

"Let's get this conference over so we can start celebrating," Beckett states.

"I thought Coach wanted to fly back home right away," I say.

Cade chuckles. "He had a change of heart."

"Yeah," Beckett chimes in. "Says it's fine if we want to stay for a couple of hours and celebrate our win, Montreal style."

"Oh my gosh. He totally wants to rub your win in the other team's face." I think back to the coach's smile from moments ago.

"Absolutely, he does, and he deserves to," Beckett says.

I press my lips in a line. "I wonder if Penny has been informed of the change of plans, yet?"

"She will definitely be the only one among us who isn't psyched for a night of partying in Montreal." Cade scoffs, shaking his head. "Not it!"

"Not it!" Beckett repeats.

"Not it for what?" I ask.

"Telling Penny about the plans," Cade states.

I look from Cade to Beckett, and they both look at me wearing mischievous expressions. "I'll tell her. She likes me. I brought her coffee."

CHAPTER TWENTY-FOUR

CADE

"Shots! Shots! Shots!" Jaden cheers, and some others join in on the chant. He wears a smile, looking pretty proud of himself, as he should be. Scores are important, but so are good defensemen. Jaden and Max put in the work tonight against Montreal and helped us secure our victory.

"Oh God..." Penelope sighs.

Beckett nudges her arm. "It's innocent fun, Pen. No worries."

Penny blows out a huff and rolls her eyes.

"You need to lighten up. You're strung way too tight." Dreven tilts his bottle of beer back and chugs.

"Are you kidding me?" Penny glares and addresses Dreven. "You're my biggest problem on this team,

Gunner. You have the coping skills of a five-year-old. Always throwing tantrums."

He narrows his stare, and his nostrils flare. He stands from the stool, and the beast that he is, he towers over everyone. "Who wants shots? Next round's on me!"

Penny's mouth drops open.

Pulling the sucker from my mouth, I toss it into a nearby garbage can and take Iris's hand. "Come on." I lead her toward the dance floor. We weave our way through dancing bodies, finding an open space in the center. Tucking a lock of hair behind her ear, I press my lips to her forehead. I wrap my arms around her waist and pull her body against mine. A current pop song blasts from the speakers around the club. It's upbeat with lots of bass. But Iris and I sway to an entirely different melody, one only we can hear.

The club is filled with hockey players and fans. Most of Montreal's players are here, and we're having a great time. As competitive as we are on the ice, we get along pretty well off it. They're good guys.

Surprisingly, Coach even celebrates. He sits at a corner table having a beer with some of the coaching staff from both Montreal's team and our own. He's smiling as if he doesn't have a care in the world when, just yesterday, I thought he would have a stroke from so much stress. Montreal's head coach,

his archnemesis, is notably absent from the celebration.

Iris circles her hand around my neck and runs her
fingers through my hair. Bending down, I kiss her
slowly as we dance. All the stars have aligned, making
this whole night feel so surreal. The only thing better
than celebrating a great win against a rival is doing so
with my lips against hers.

My body hums with hers next to mine, and my lips
move with more fervor, greedy to taste her. "I can't
wait to get home," I say on an exhale before my tongue
circles with hers again.

Since we've made our relationship official, we
haven't spent a night apart.

She pulls her mouth from mine and runs her
tongue along my lips. "You taste like pineapple." She
nibbles at my bottom lip. "I'm ready to leave. I want to
be home, too."

I can hear the need in her voice, and I know exactly
how she's feeling because I feel the same way.

We continue to sway in our own little lust bubble
amid a crowd of energetic sweaty people. Our vibe,
different from everyone else's, is on its own level. Iris
tightens the hold on my neck and pulls my face tighter
against hers. Our breath meets, our tongues dance, and
our moans caress.

Iris glides her hands down my chest. Our mouths

still connected, her hand slides south until her fingers inch under my waistband.

Pulling my lips from hers, I grab her wrist and move it away. "No."

Her pout makes me grin.

I wouldn't be the first Cranes player to get a handy in the middle of a crowded bar, and I certainly wouldn't be the last. But we can't. We're both here because of jobs we love. I'm not risking her reputation or job for it. Not to mention, when Iris makes me come, it will be loud and explosive. It's not something I care to keep quiet.

I thread my fingers through hers. "Come on."

We exit the dance floor and slip away from the rest of the group. "Where are we going?" Iris whispers.

"I have no idea." I lead her down a dimly lit hall-way. We pass the restrooms and the door to the kitchen.

There's a door at the end of the hallway. Pushing it open, I peek in. Score.

I pull Iris inside and lock the door behind us. The oversized closet is a pantry of sorts with metal shelves lined full of extra linens, to-go containers, bulk condi-ments, and pallets of shrink-wrapped glassware.

I push her back against the locked door and crash my mouth to hers. Now that taking her is imminent, the need is that much greater. Iris groans in my mouth.

Threading her fingers through my hair, she pulls me in close. She drops her hands and starts unbuttoning my jeans. This time, I let her.

She drops to her knees, grabs ahold of my jeans, and pulls them and my boxers down my legs, freeing me. Without a word, she covers my shaft with her warm mouth. Splaying one hand against the door, I steady myself. My free hand grips Iris's hair and guides her over my length in a perfect rhythm. My mouth falls open, and my head falls back. Eyes closed, I take in the sensations. The thumping music from the club is loud, even in here, drowning out my groans.

Iris takes me all the way into her mouth, and my tip hits the back of her throat. She cups my balls, massaging them with one hand, and I start to lose control.

Taking a step back, I pull away from her, not wanting to finish yet. Scooping my hands under her arms, I lift her from the ground. "My turn." I kiss her mouth before dropping to my knees.

I push her skirt up to her waist and pull off her thong. She leans her back against the door, and I lift one of her legs over my shoulder, opening her wide for me. My tongue licks up her slit, and she cries out, grasping my hair. Two fingers enter her wet opening and slide against her front wall as I lick and suck her clit.

"Oh God," she moans, her legs already shaking.

I'm so desperate to have her fall apart, to taste her release and feel her crumple. I lick harder as I hand fuck her, moving my fingers against the spot that drives her wild.

She's panting, pulling at my hair, her pelvis moving to meet my hand. She cries out and bends at the waist as her body starts convulsing. Splaying my free hand against her waist, I hold her upright against the door. She moans as her orgasm courses through her.

When her trembling subsides, I remove my fingers. After moving my tongue up her slit one more time, I stand.

I hold her face in my hands and kiss her hard. She clings to my shoulders and moves her tongue against mine. I twist us both so my back is against the door, and I push the small of her back. "Grab your ankles and spread wide for me." My command is a husky whisper.

Iris complies, and I slide inside her. We release a collective groan of pleasure. I fist her hips and pull her back onto me as I plunge forward. This position hits so deep, it causes us both to cry out. "Oh fuck, baby." I pound into her again and again. Everything around us fades away. The music disappears, and the containers on the shelves beside us evaporate. All I can feel is pleasure. All I can hear is the evidence of her own. All I can see is my hands on the side of her ass as I move in and out of her opening. It's fucking heaven. I pull her against me as I thrust deep inside her. The pleasure inside me builds.

"Touch yourself," I groan out.

Iris puts a hand between her legs and works her clit. My chest rises and falls with heavy breaths. My orgasm is burning, ready to explode, but I need her to fall with me.

She whimpers and cries out as she comes. I push deep inside her and let my release go as her walls spasm around me, sucking every last drop from me. I fall back against the door as the final tremors of my release course through me.

Iris moves forward, and I fall from her opening. She stands and turns toward me. Leaning her cheek against my chest, we catch our breaths, breathing hard. After a minute, I pull up my jeans, and Iris gets her skirt and panties situated. She leans up and gives me a peck of a kiss.

I take her face between my hands and rub my thumbs over her skin. "I'm obsessed with you," I tell her.

She grins. "I'm pretty addicted to you if we're being honest."

"That was so good, Rosie. I never knew it could be that good."

"Believe me, normally it's not. It's that good because it's us."

Leaning down, I move my lips against hers.

She peppers quick kisses against my mouth. "I'm so glad you didn't make me wait until we got home."

"You and me both." I grab her ass, and she yelps. "We should get back, though, before Beck comes looking for us."

"I'm ready to go home. I want you inside me until we fall asleep from exhaustion and pleasure."

I chuckle. "Me too. Let me go put a bug in Coach's ear." I give her a wink and unlock the door.

A server reaching for the door handle when I swing it open yelps in surprise. Her eyes go wide as she looks from me to Iris. "Sorry, we got lost. We're looking for the bathroom?" Iris says.

The server blinks twice and points down the hall.

"Thanks." Iris grins, and we hurry from the pantry.

CHAPTER
TWENTY-FIVE

CADE

I slide my shirt over my head. It sticks as I slide it down, my skin still a little damp from the shower.

Coach walks by. "Good practice today, Richards."

"Thanks, Coach." I give him a wave as he continues through the locker room.

It was a great practice. Everything felt good. My body cooperated, and my plays worked. The puck went where I wanted it to go, when I wanted it there. That's a rarity, for sure.

I toss all my things into my duffel, then grab the last thing left in my locker, my phone.

My heart stutters when I see several missed calls from Margaret's residence community. I put my cell to my ear and play the voicemails. The nurses who left the messages aren't very forthcoming with information, only telling me that I need to come to the home as soon as possible.

With a hike of my duffel onto my shoulder, I hurry out of the locker room, letting Beckett know I'm going to see Margaret.

In the hallway leading to the offices, I pass Penny. "Have you seen Iris?"

"She's out meeting with vendors. Is there something I can help you with?"

"No, I'm good. Thanks." I hurry past her.

I call the facility as soon as I'm clear of the building and in my car. I'm transferred to Margaret's nurse. The only thing she tells me is that Margaret isn't doing well. I tell her I'm on the way.

Loud music blares through my car speakers, and I zone out on the way to see my mom. I can't get all worked up before I know what's going on. However, they've never called me in like this, so I feel it's much more serious than they want to tell me over the phone. I tried to visit Margaret last week, but she was having a bad day and didn't want visitors, which happens quite a bit. It must be scary not knowing who you are or what you're doing. I'm sure the last thing I'd want to do if I felt that way is visit with a stranger. The lack of a visit last week didn't sting as much since two weeks prior, I'd visited with Iris and we'd had a good time.

A few blocks away from the facility, I call Iris, but she doesn't pick up. I don't leave her a message. It's probably best to wait to see what I'm dealing with before I worry her.

I park and hurry inside. Per normal, I sign in and tell the receptionist I'm here to see Margaret. She looks at me, gives me a terse nod, and instructs me to have a seat. I only have time to walk to the waiting area before the doctor calls my name.

"Mr. Richards? Margaret's son?" she questions. The doctor must be new. She's not one I've seen before.

"Yes, that's me."

She motions me forward and starts walking down the hallway toward Margaret's room. I follow. Stopping, she turns to face me. With a look to either side, she plasters a mix of a frown and a smile onto her face and holds my stare. In a hushed voice, she says, "I'm afraid Margaret's health has taken a turn for the worse. She's very ill, and I don't think she has much longer. We called you in so you could say goodbye."

"What do you mean? I was here a few weeks ago, and she was fine? What exactly is wrong with her? Are you running tests? There has to be something you can do."

She does that weird smile frown thing again.

"We've run blood work and brain scans. Nothing is showing up for us to treat. Unfortunately, we see this sometimes in dementia patients. There's nothing technically wrong, but their health fades nonetheless. Margaret is up there in age, and it may just be her time. I'm very sorry. If there was anything we could do to help her, we would. But there's just not."

That answer isn't going to fly. If she's ill, then they need to fix her. But I can't argue about that right now. I need to see her. With a shake of my head, I move past the doctor and into Margaret's room.

She's lying in bed with her eyes closed, and I suck in a breath. She looks twenty years older than she did a few short weeks ago. She's pale and appears to have lost weight. I hardly recognize her.

Tears spring to my eyes, and I rush over to her bed. "Mom," I choke. Sitting at her bedside, I hold her hand in mine. Tears fall, and I don't try to stop them. I knew I wouldn't have Margaret forever. That's been painfully obvious over the past few years as I lost her bit by bit each day. It was devastating to watch her lose her mind and memories, and maybe I was being selfish, but it still brought comfort to be able to see her, in physical form, at least. And when she recalled stories about me, like she did when Iris was here, it gave me a respite from mourning her and brought a sliver of joy. Those fragments of clarity, while few and far between, gave me hope and made me feel as if I hadn't already lost her.

The truth is, I lost her years ago. When you really love someone, loss is hard to process. Denial and false hopes are so much easier to stomach.

"I'm sorry," I choke out, bringing her frail, wrinkled hand to my face. I kiss her hand and hold it to my cheeks, apologizing again. I'm not sure what I'm apologizing for, but it's safe to say everything. I'm sorry that she lost her memories. I'm sorry that she spent the last few years of her life not knowing who she was, who I was, or that I loved her. I'm sorry that she's dying, and I'm sorry I can't do anything about it.

As much as I want to fight with the doctors and demand they do something, nothing can be done. Deep down, I know that to be true.

So many things in life are just so fucking unfair. I knew that well, and at ten years old, Margaret was the first person in my life to show me that life isn't all bad. We didn't have much, she and I, but we had love. We had a modest life with lots of little wiener dogs, laughter, acceptance, and unconditional love. I couldn't have asked for a better parent.

"Cade?" she says my name, her voice weak.

I open my eyes wide and look at her. I'm afraid to blink, sure I'm dreaming. She holds my stare, her tired eyes waiting for a response. "You remember me?" My tears fall harder.

"I could never forget you." She pulls our joined hands to her lips and kisses my hand. "What's wrong, my boy?"

I shake my head and swallow the emotion in my throat. I don't know how long I have her for. "I don't want to lose you."

"You'll never lose me." She looks around the room, and her brows furrow in confusion. Her face falls, and heartbreak lines her features. "You already have, haven't you?" A tear falls down her cheek. "Where am I?" Her voice is weak.

"It's a home for people who've lost their memories. We picked it out together."

She nods, closing her eyes. She takes in a deep breath and opens her eyes. "Tell me about your hockey. Tell me about your life. I want to know everything I've missed."

I give her a quick rundown of college and getting drafted to the Cranes with Beckett. I tell her that I'm dating Iris and that the two of us came to visit her a few weeks ago.

"You made all your dreams come true." The corners of her lips tilt up. "Tell me, my boy. Are you happy?"

I choke back a sob and nod. I still can't believe I'm talking to her, and she's talking to me.

She grunts, pushing her arms to her sides, and tries to move but is unsuccessful. "Can you please pull me to the side of the bed? I want you to lie with me."

I do as instructed and climb into bed with her. The bed is bigger than a typical hospital bed as the room is made to look like an apartment. I'd guess it's a full-sized bed. Side by side, we both fit comfortably. Margaret leans her head against my shoulder and holds my hand. "All I ever wanted was for you to find happiness." She squeezes my hand. "You made your momma's heart happy."

"I don't understand why this is happening. It's not fair. I don't want to lose you."

She sighs. "There are some things we'll never be able to explain, my dear. Life is unfair. What you went through as a boy is unfair. It makes no sense. The only thing I can say is that life is a complex journey. One that I wish didn't contain so many lows, but it's the hard parts in life that make the highs so sweet. The sad makes us so grateful for the happy."

"They say you're dying, Mom. What hurts? What can I do? I can find a doctor who will help."

"I think they're right," she says matter-of-factly. "I feel different. Tired." It's quiet for a moment before she says, "From the look of things, it doesn't seem like I've been doing much living lately. Dying might be best. Maybe heaven needs me."

"I need you," I choke. "There's so much I haven't done. So much I want you to see. You deserve so much more."

I can hear the smile in her soft voice. "I got everything I deserve the day I got you. I've already been so blessed. You know how much I love you, Cade, right? You know how incredible of a person you are? You are the most beautiful gift I've ever received, and you made my life infinitely happier." She swallows and pulls in a long breath. "I know I've told you, but I prayed for you. I dreamed of you. You were the missing piece of my heart, and when the social worker brought you to my house that day, I felt whole for the first time. That kind of love doesn't fade. It surpasses time and space. I'll love you forever whether I'm on this earth or not. You better believe that I'll be loving you for eternity. What I need, my boy, is for you to promise me something."

"What?"

"I need you to promise me you'll love yourself. Always. If you do that, happiness will follow because you, Cade, are impossible not to love. Will you promise me that?"

"I promise." I clear my throat, pushing down the emotion as more tears escape from my eyes. "I'm not ready for you to leave me."

With a little effort, she turns to her side and places

her hand on my heart. "I never will. I'll always be here."

My lip trembles. "I love you. You saved me."

"All I did was love you. You saved yourself." Her soft voice is barely audible. "I'm so tired. I'm gonna rest for just a minute."

"Okay, you rest." I kiss the top of her head. "I love you," I tell her again, wanting her to hear it because she won't know who I am when she wakes.

But she doesn't wake.

She dies beside me twenty minutes later, her hand on my heart.

As painful as the past few minutes have been, they were an incredible gift. She knew I needed her one more time. I don't know how she did it, but she came back so I could say goodbye.

Somehow, two hours have passed, and I don't remember much of it. Paperwork had to be signed and stuff arranged. I vaguely remember speaking to someone from the funeral home when they came to pick up Margaret's body. I'm told I arranged to have her things moved to my storage facility, where most of her belongings are already being kept. According to my cell phone history, I've spoken to Beckett.

Sitting on the stone bench in the courtyard, I stare at the frozen pond. During the warmer months, a whole family of ducks and swans live here. Mom loved sitting out here and watching the birds carry on, dipping their heads underwater to catch fish, trying to navigate the water with their line of ducklings. She found them amusing.

Now, they're somewhere south for the winter, and the pond is ice. It's sad really.

Someone clears their throat from behind me. "Mr. Richards. Are you okay? Can we call someone to be with you?"

Peering over my shoulder, I see one of the nursing aides who was quite fond of Margaret. Her face is tight with worry. I imagine her heart is hurting too. She spent more time with Margaret over the past few years than I did. The staff here really are incredible. They dedicate their lives to making sure elderly people, like my mom, have the best care and highest quality of life possible during their final days. It has to be a taxing occupation, both physically and emotionally. I make a mental note to send thank-you gifts to the staff for caring for my mom the best they could.

Looking down toward my hands, I realize I can no longer feel them. I've been sitting out here freezing, and I didn't even realize it. No wonder the aide is concerned.

I stand from the bench and turn to leave. There's no reason to stick around here anymore. My mother is gone.

"Thank you for taking such good care of her. It means more to me than you will ever know," I say to the aide as I walk past.

In my car, I'm equally as lost as I was on the bench. I'm not quite sure what to do with myself. I suppose I should continue with life as normal, but how does one just go on? A beloved part of my life is simply gone, and I don't know how to make sense of that.

Pulling up the social media app that I never use, I search for Iris. She reminded me last week that I can see where she is whenever I want as the app has location sharing. The little cartoon version of herself shows up, and when I zoom in, I see she's at her parents' house. I start driving in her direction, having an overwhelming need to be with someone who loves me. I need her.

As I approach her parents' home, I take in the scene before me. Iris's car is parked in the driveway, and right behind it is a BMW I've seen before. To the side of the vehicles, a pair stands, holding each other in an embrace. If my heart was working, it would surely be feeling something. When I drive by the house slowly, it's clear the couple with arms wrapped around one another is Iris and her ex Ben. The exchange could be innocent or the opposite of. It doesn't really matter, though. The fact is, I need her, and she's comforting someone else.

Hitting the gas, I drive past.

CHAPTER
TWENTY-SIX

IRIS

"I'm really sorry, babe." Ben releases his grip on me, allowing me to step away from his hug.

He showed up unannounced and caught me off guard. It's my first time seeing him since he was inside Nancy. I knew this day would eventually come. We run in the same circles, so I couldn't avoid him forever. I didn't plan to be ambushed in the driveway, however.

I'm surprised at how little his presence affects me. I spent a year of my life with him, only to come to a shocking and abrupt end. I thought when I did eventually see him again, I'd feel... something. Sadness. Pain. Heartbreak. Yet the truth is, I feel none of those things. In truth, I feel annoyed. It's been a hectic day at work in which I've spent the entirety of it running errands and meeting with people. I'm exhausted. I just wanted to stop off at my parents, grab some things that I need, and head over to Cade's. I'm too tired to deal with Ben right now.

"It's fine. It's in the past." I eye his car, hoping he gets the hint that he can leave now. All is forgiven.

"No." He shakes his head. "It's not fine. I shouldn't have cheated on you. It wasn't you. I was all in with you. I'd been sleeping with Nancy for years... I guess it was habit. Something I did to relieve stress. It didn't mean anything."

Oh great, he cheated on me for the entirety of our relationship. That's always something a girl wants to hear. I narrow my gaze and take Ben in. While attractive, he's obviously a self-centered asshole and always has been. Clearly, my time with him was in my self-sabotage period. What was I thinking?

I clear my throat. "Is there something you need, Ben? I have to be somewhere."

"Yeah," he huffs. "I need you."

I furrow my brows. "It's been weeks, and this is the first time you've reached out." I scoff with a shake of my head. "Are you just feeling regret now?"

He shrugs. "I wasn't sure what I wanted."

Translation—he needed to screw dozens of women while he was uncommitted.

"Look, Ben, if I'm being honest… you did me a favor. I was never meant to be with you."

His mouth falls open and then closes again. I can't believe I've rendered Benjamin Stormberg Junior speechless. It's a good feeling. For a year of my life, I had to listen to this man talk. Now he can listen to me.

"I don't need your apologies. I don't want your promises. The only thing I need is for you to move your car because I have somewhere to be."

"Iris, I think that you and I—"

I cut him off, finishing the sentence for him. "Are through. Please go."

His brows furrow, and his nostrils flare. "You aren't going to find better than me, Iris."

"I already did. A word of advice, you should probably do some serious self-reflection before your next relationship because, as things are going right now, you'll never be truly happy. And I'm telling you… real happiness is amazing." I step around him and slide into the front seat of my car without waiting for his response.

Pushing the ignition button, I wait for him to move out from behind me. He turns one way out of the drive, and I head in the other direction. I don't so much as look for him in my rearview mirror. Not a cell in my body will miss his presence.

The drive to Cade's condo doesn't take long, and I

can't wait to see him. Being out of the office today made me miss him like crazy. Normally, I get to pop into practice to watch him and the guys play for a bit or see him in the halls. A day without any Cade sightings is a sad one.

Cade doesn't answer his door or my texts. I wait outside his condo for almost an hour, and I have no idea where he is. I check his location on social media, but his avatar doesn't appear. His phone must be dead. I leave him a couple of text messages telling him to call me, and I head back to my parents' house.

I'm sure there's a simple explanation for Cade's lack of communication yesterday, and undoubtedly, I'm overreacting. But as I race into work an hour early, I have a sinking feeling that something is very wrong. Cade and I have spent every evening together since we became official weeks ago. It isn't like him to ghost me.

I hurry to the weight room and scan the machines for Cade. I don't see him but I do see Beckett which calms my nerves. If something were really wrong, Beckett would be at Cade's side.

"Where's Cade?" I ask my brother, trying to keep my voice steady.

"He's taking a personal day for obvious reasons." Beckett sets the weights down with a grunt.

"What reasons?"

Beckett looks confused. "Margaret."

"What about Margaret?"

"When's the last time you spoke to Cade? You didn't hear that Margaret died?" he asks with knitted brows.

"What?" I gasp. "When? Why didn't he tell me? I tried to get ahold of him all night."

Beckett shrugs. "Yesterday, and maybe he just needs some space."

He doesn't need space. He needs me. Turning away from my brother, I stop in the offices and let Penny know that I'm taking a day off.

I call Cade again and again as I drive to his condo. Each time, the call goes straight to voicemail. Outside his place, I pound my fist against his door and still no answer. A scan of the parking lot confirms he isn't here. His car is nowhere in sight.

If he's not home, where is he?

I rack my brain to think of where he'd go when he's hurting, and it dawns on me. Back in my car, I speed toward Margaret's old house. Cade had all the contents removed and put into storage with the intention of selling the place when Margaret was admitted into the assisted living facility, but he couldn't go through with it. As far as I know, the house has sat empty for several years now.

I sigh with relief when I turn the corner onto Margaret's street, and Cade's car comes into view. I park beside his car and hurry inside.

"Cade?" I call into the empty house, and my voice echoes off the barren walls.

He doesn't answer, but I find him sitting on the hardwood floor, his back up against the living room wall. He's awake, though prominent purple bags sit under his eyes. He lifts the half-empty bottle of booze in his hand. "There you are! How's Ben?"

How's Ben? What is he even talking about?

My heart sinks. "Did you drive by my house yesterday?"

His head falls forward, and it takes him a second to bring it back up. "Sure did. Looks like you and the ex are getting awfully close again. Perfect timing really. I mean, I've lost everything anyway." His words are slurred.

With a sigh, I head into the kitchen and find a plastic cup in the cupboard. To my relief, the water still works. I return to Cade with a glass of water and trade it out for the liquor bottle. "Drink this."

Cade downs the glass of water, and I get him another. He drinks that one, too. Sitting down beside him, I take his hand in mine and lean my head against his shoulder. "I am so sorry about your mom, Cade. I'm so sorry I wasn't there for you, but you have to know nothing is going on between Ben and me. He gave me a hug, and then I shut him down and asked him to leave. I don't miss him. I don't want him. I love you, and I know you know that."

"Yeah." Cade releases a sad exhale. "I don't know how to handle this type of grief."

"One day at a time." I straddle his lap and wrap my arms around him. "Come here." I pull him to me.

He circles his arms around my back and buries his head against my neck and cries.

We sit in this embrace for some time. I hold him tight as he clings to me and releases his agony. My heart breaks more knowing he came to me in the midst of his devastation and found my arms around Ben. It makes me hate Ben that much more.

He sits back, his arms still around my waist, and he stares at me with bloodshot eyes. "He's a lawyer like you. He comes from a family like yours. I'll understand."

It takes me a second to realize what he's talking about, and my heart twists in pain, knowing that, even now, Cade still feels as if he's not enough.

I hold his face in my hands and wait until his hazel eyes lock with mine. "You listen to me, Cade Richards. You are the greatest man I've ever known. I am so lucky to call you mine. No one in this entire world could ever mean to me what you do. You have made me happier than I've ever been in my life. I choose you now. I choose you tomorrow. And I'll choose you forever. Please believe that."

"I'm sorry. I'm just so fucked up."

"It's okay." I press my lips to his. The kiss is short, but I pour all my love into it. I want Cade to feel it all.

"She was just all I had. You know? I don't know how to live in a world without her." A tear falls down his face.

I pepper kisses over his tear-soaked face, wanting to kiss away his agony. "She loved you very much, Cade. But she's not all you have. You have so many people who love you because you are so worthy of love. You have your team, your coach, Beckett, and you have me. I love you." I kiss his cheek. "I love you." I kiss his forehead. "I love you." I trail kisses down his other cheek, stopping at his mouth. "I love you," I say against his lips in the space where our breath is shared —where we're one.

"I love you," he answers, his voice hoarse. He pulls me against him, hugging me tight.

"Come on," I urge. Sliding off his lap, I stand and extend my hand.

"Where are we going?" He takes my hand and stumbles to his feet.

I hitch my arm through his and steady him as he walks. "I'm going to take you home. I'm going to feed you, and bathe you, and love you while you process your loss. You're not alone, my sweet Dummy. With me, you'll never be alone. Okay?"

"Okay, Rosie girl. Okay." His voice cracks.

He leans in and kisses my forehead, and I know we'll be okay.

CHAPTER
TWENTY-SEVEN

CADE

I'm in utter awe at how many people attended Margaret's funeral. I loved the woman so much, it was easy to feel as if I was the only one. But her love was endless, and the lives she touched, numerous.

There are dozens of people—all seemingly happy, well-adjusted adults—she fostered before me that she kept in touch with over the years. I can't help but feel pride that Margaret's love and guidance during a difficult time in their lives helped them grow into the people they are now.

Her neighbors, friends, people from church, her dachshund community, and employees from local businesses she frequented have all shown, too. She left a lasting light wherever she went.

I look out onto the faces in the congregation, and my heart warms seeing every person in the Cranes organization here as well. My fellow players, coaches, equipment managers, doctors, physical therapists, and office staff have taken the day off to celebrate the woman who raised me.

Iris is right; there are a lot of people in my corner. She smiles from the pew. Her warmth radiates, giving me strength as I prepare for the eulogy. She's been my rock this past week, and I'm so grateful to have her.

The night of Margaret's death was rough, and I was in a very dark place. The brain is powerful, and paired with grief, it can be debilitating. The moment I allowed Iris in, letting her take care of me and carry some of my sadness, everything got better. I will always love Margaret. I'll forever be grateful for her love. And I'll always miss her. But she is in a better place where her mind is her own.

I hold the notecards in my hand and look out at the crowd of people as I talk. I recall anecdotes of life with Margaret, comical and heartwarming recollections that highlight what an amazing person she was. The group smiles through tears as the stories touch their hearts.

Continuing, I give my final thoughts. "When I started to plan for this eulogy and really began to think about my life with my mom, so many vivid memories came to mind. The hardest part about writing this was deciding which stories to include. And that got me thinking about what an incredible life one must have lived to instill so many beautiful memories into someone else that it's nearly impossible to choose just a couple to share. For those of you here who knew Margaret, I'm sure you have your own memories to share. She was an incredible woman, and she made the world a better place. We're all better humans because she loved us. She literally changed my life. She will live on through me because everything I am, I learned from her. She saved me when others cast me aside. She was so many things to so many people. But to me, she'll always be the first person who made me feel as if I belonged. She loved me unconditionally, and I will miss her for the rest of my life."

I leave the notecards on the pulpit. I didn't look at them once, not needing to. I was afraid I'd be too emotional to remember what I wanted to say, but staring down at a bunch of people who will carry Margaret's light with them, just as I will, gave me a deep sense of peace.

As I walk off the stage and down the aisle, the string quartet plays as a video montage of Margaret's life displays on the big screen in the front of the space. Iris helped me go through Margaret's old box of photos in storage to put together a visually beautiful send-off.

I stand just outside the exit and personally thank everyone who came to celebrate her life.

After the service, we all meet for a luncheon I've set up at Margaret's favorite restaurant. So many stories from her past are shared, and it's a special experience.

When the night winds down and everyone is gone except Iris and Beckett, they tell me to change out of my suit and into something comfortable.

"Why?" I quirk a brow.

"Just do it, bro," Beckett insists.

I put on a pair of sweatpants and get into the car with Beckett and Iris. They share secret looks with one another. "What do you two have planned?" I lean back against the seat of the car with a yawn.

"Don't worry, you'll like it. I promise." Iris grins.

We pull into the movie theater.

"We're going to see a movie?" I ask.

We exit the car, and Iris grabs my hand. "You'll see."

The lobby is empty, which I find odd, but I don't ask questions and allow Iris to lead the way. We enter a movie theater, and within it is every member of the Cranes organization. It's a large theater with leather recliner seats. There are tables of candy, popcorn, and drinks lining the theater's walls. My eyes are damp with emotion at the sight of the tubs of Dum Dums suckers at the end of every aisle of seats, a nod to

Margaret's candy dishes that were never without the suckers.

"You guys." A smile finds my face.

"So…" Beckett clears his throat and raises his voice so everyone can hear. "We didn't want you to be alone tonight after such an emotional day. We rented out the theater and will be playing a collection of Jim Carrey movies, starting with *Liar Liar*."

"No!" I clap my hands together and laugh, my eyes welling with tears. "You guys…" I'm at a loss for words. Jim Carrey was Margaret's favorite actor, and growing up, we watched his movies on repeat. Her favorite was *Liar Liar*, and I have vivid memories of her explosive laughter the first time she watched that film.

"What do you think?" Iris asks.

"I think I can't believe Coach is out past eight on the eve of a game day," I call over to Coach Albright, who gives me a thumbs-up. "No, but seriously. You guys… this is great. The way you all showed up for me this past week, today especially, I can't thank you enough. I'm really grateful to be part of the Cranes family."

Hollers and cheers sound off, and a round of "We love you, Heartbreaker!" echoes throughout the space.

"You guys, I need a new name." I pull Iris to my side.

Beckett scoffs and gives my arm a playful punch.

"You know that ain't happening," he says to me before addressing the others in a raised voice. "Get your snacks and drinks. The movie will start in ten minutes."

Iris dishes up a tub of popcorn, grabs a bottle of Sprite and a package of Sour Patch Kids, and we head toward the seats. I grab two handfuls of suckers at the end of the row, and we make our way to the three chairs that say "reserved."

Beckett saved the three chairs in the center, middle of the theater, for us. "Thanks, man," I say.

"Only the best." He grins.

We get situated in our seats. I extend the leg rest out as far as it will go and lean back. The lights dim, and the movie starts.

While today was never going to be fun, I'd say it went as well as it could. There was so much love shared, both past and present, it's hard not to feel grateful. For everything.

And at this moment especially, laughter. Mixed with a room of people who love me, it may just be the best medicine.

CHAPTER
TWENTY-EIGHT

IRIS

Contrary to my first week on the job, planning elegant galas where we raise an enormous amount of money for charity is actually a small portion of my job. Most projects are easy meet and greets, setting up interviews with local sports media, and photo shoots with fans. After planning each several times, I could do it in my sleep. I'm not complaining as I'm still vastly happier than I was at the firm—admittedly for more reasons than one.

My relationship with Cade has survived the second half of the season. Now, late April, Cade and I have been going strong for over three months. Most days, I still can't believe it's real and that I'm truly this happy. It seems like a dream. Life hasn't been all positive.

We've gone through some tough losses both on and off the ice, but our connection made all the hard times easier. I keep waiting for the bubble to burst that will send me careening down to earth where reality awaits. But just maybe, this HEA is forever.

Clipboard in hand, I watch as Cade bends on one knee to talk to a little boy who came to get photos with him. His smile is infectious and radiates pure joy. The entire team is on a high, having ranked in the top sixteen. They're moving on to the Stanley Cup playoffs and are feeling good. They have every right to feel confident as they've performed better this season than they have in years.

"Do you play hockey?" Cade asks the boy who can't be more than seven years old as he signs a jersey.

The boy nods, wide-eyed and starstruck.

"What's your favorite position?" Cade hands him the jersey.

The boy just stares back, his mouth unmoving.

"I know. It's hard to decide, right? They're all a blast. That's the cool thing about being your age. You can play them all and just have fun. Do you want a picture?" Cade questions.

The boy is still speechless, so his mother answers, "We would love one."

"Absolutely." Cade stays on one knee so he's on the boy's level and turns to face the camera.

Beckett steps up beside me and bumps me with his shoulder. "I don't know who is more awestruck, you or that kid." He chuckles.

Turning away from Cade, I give Beck a mock glare. "I'm just doing my job."

"Yeah, if your job is ogling Heartbreaker." He scoffs.

I purse my lips and raise a brow. "I'm not ogling him. Just making sure everything runs smoothly."

"Okay." He grins. "Look, I'm happy for you, Sis. Truly. I mean, it's about time for both of you to be happy. But do you think you can peel your eyes off him for two seconds to help me? This fan says she paid for a picture and a signed jersey, but we don't have the jersey in the pile and can't find evidence of the purchase on the list."

"Sure, what's her name?" I sneak another glance Cade's way before turning to follow Beckett and flip through the master list attached to my clipboard.

I love my job.

"My love," Cade says with a sigh. "I've already told you I trust you. Whatever you want."

This is as close as Cade comes to complaining, and

it's cute, but he's not getting out of this. "No, you have to live there, and I want it to reflect your style, too. Your home's decor should make you feel content and bring you peace."

"But you have better taste than I do. You know what I like. And I'm tired."

I slide my hand into his and pull him into the furniture store. I know the guy is beat, but I also realize that if we don't make a final decision on this sofa, it could be another two months before we have the chance to get back here. We're in the very short window between the regular season and the two-month elimination playoffs. Ideally, the Cranes will make it to the Stanley Cup finals in June.

The sixteen teams begin the best of seven elimination tournament next week, and Coach has them training extremely hard. I empathize with Cade, but we haven't had a sofa in a month. It was donated when we, and by *we*, I mean me, started the condo renovation last month. It's taken me this long to coordinate a time to get him here. We don't have a lot of free time to relax and watch TV, but for the past month, when we do, we're sitting in camping chairs I took from my parents' garage. It's time for a new sofa.

For all intents and purposes, Cade's condo is my home now, too. Considering I've slept there every night for months and store all my belongings there, it's safe to say I live there. The past several months have been a whirlwind, and perhaps we've moved a little fast. I think we've both wanted the other for so long that as soon as we got together, we went all in.

Leading Cade to a leather navy-blue sectional, I say, "This was the one I was leaning toward."

Over the past few months, as I've started making changes, Cade's stark-white walls have been painted a soft grayish blue. The accents around the home are mainly a deep blue, white, and gray. The color pallet is clean and crisp while bringing a calm and soothing vibe to the space. It isn't too masculine or feminine, and quite honestly, I think it fits us both perfectly. Cade says he agrees, but I want to make sure.

"Perfect. Sold. Let's go." He squeezes my hand.

I extend my arm toward the sofa. "Sit. You don't even know if it's comfortable," I protest, the skin around my eyes crinkle with amusement.

Releasing my hand, he falls onto the navy-blue faux leather. He closes his eyes and exhales. "Sold. I could fall asleep right now."

"Do you like the color?" I ask.

"Yep. Love it."

"The style?"

"Perfect."

"Dummy," I grumble.

Cade laughs. "You know what I lived in before you

came along, right? I was perfectly happy with zero decoration. Heck, I'm fine with the camping chairs we have now. I promise I'm good with whatever you choose."

I extend my hand, and Cade takes it. I go through the motions of pulling him up, though I do little to actually help. He stands on his own. "Let me show you the other one I thought you would like."

"Okay."

Cade follows me around the store as I show him the pieces I've been eyeing. He feigns interest and agrees with my recommendations. When I mention trying the feel of another sofa, he stops in his tracks.

"Iris?"

I put the blue swirled stained glass vase down on the display end table and turn to face Cade. "Yeah?"

"Do you love me?"

"You know I do." I take a step toward him.

"Then, for the love of God, please make the decor decisions, and believe me when I say I'll love whatever you choose."

"But…" I start to protest.

Cade quirks a brow. "Have we ever fought since we started dating?"

"No." I shake my head.

He retrieves his wallet and pulls out a credit card, handing it to me. "Well, we're about to if I don't get out of this store. I'm so exhausted. I just want to go home. Please order what you want. I'll be in the car."

He wears a look of desperation, and if I'm not mistaken, his voice trembles a little with his declaration. "Okay." I press my lips in a line and hold in a chuckle. The poor guy looks so forlorn it's comical. "I'm sorry. You know I just want you to be happy." I stand on my toes and plant a kiss on his lips.

"I have you." He holds my face between his hands and kisses my forehead. "I couldn't be anything but."

"Go wait in the car. I'll be speedy."

"Deal," he agrees, and for the first time since we stepped foot in this store, his smile is genuine.

I quickly order the original navy-blue sectional and a few decorative pieces I was eyeing and schedule the delivery. As I walk out to the car, I place an online take-out order at Cade's favorite Italian restaurant.

Another thing that's changed since I've been living with Cade is that our refrigerator is always full with healthy options and staples to make meals. But my man needs extra carbs and fast. So takeout it is.

"All done?" he asks when I return to the car.

"Yep. In five days, we'll have a beautiful new sofa and some extra decorative accessories."

"Great." He starts up the car.

Reaching over the center console, I place my hand

on his thigh. "Can you stop at Giovanni's on the way home? I placed a dinner order."

His head dips back, and he exhales through a grin. "Uh, I love you. That sounds great. Did you order the three-meat lasagna, tiramisu, and raspberry cheesecake?"

"Of course. I know your order by now. And I ordered extra breadsticks." I lower my voice with the last sentence, saying it in a seductive tone.

"You're perfect. You know that?" He steals a glance my way before turning onto the road. "I love doing life with you."

"Same."

CHAPTER
TWENTY-NINE

CADE

"Richards and Feldmore, I'm talking to you! Stay out of the penalty box!" Coach uses his pregame pep talk to warn Beckett and me about fighting.

From a coach's perspective, I get it. The first round of the playoff games has been on the crazy side. As division champs, we're playing the wildcard team, which happens to be Pittsburgh. Going into the games, we thought we'd win the first four games, making it a clean sweep. We've had an incredible season compared to Pittsburgh. No one saw it coming down to the final game. We're tied, each team securing a three-game win. The winner of today's game moves on.

It helps that today's game is home, but in reality, we

shouldn't be here. We should've already secured our spot in round two. The fact that Pittsburgh has made it to game seven is unreal. Their team is young and comprised of a bunch of hotheaded assholes. We've had more fights and spent more time in the penalty box these past six games than we have all season. At least, it's felt like it. Pittsburgh plays dirty and initiates chaos.

What makes hockey so fun to watch is the unpredictability. While the Cranes should be mopping the floor with this team, we're not. We've made some mistakes this past week, for sure. It doesn't help that the last win Pittsburgh secured was with a goal they made in a powerplay move when Beck and I were in the penalty box, leaving our team outnumbered.

Pulling in steady breaths, I calm my nerves as we make our way to the ice. I can't let the fuckers on the opposing team get under my skin today.

"Finding your Zen?" Beckett chuckles.

"Trying to."

"Me too. We have to keep our heads today. Those assholes don't deserve to move on. We do."

"Hell yeah, we do."

I've been playing with the Cranes for four years, and this is the best we've been. We've worked hard to get here, and the guys on this team deserve to go all the way and win the Cup.

"We got this." Beckett holds out his gloved hand, and I bump it with mine as we step onto the ice to an arena full of cheering Cranes fans. The stands are a sea of navy-blue jerseys.

I hold my fist to my chest, tapping the white number ten on my chest for good luck before pumping my fist in the air. The crowd of fans, especially those wearing the number ten go wild, pumping their fists.

The number ten has always been my number. It's the age I was when everything in my life turned around for the better. It was a great year, the number ten, a lucky one. As I skate around the ice in warm-up, I think of everything I've gone through to get here, all the people who have supported me along the way, the fans who show up every home game and cheer so loud they lose their voices, Coach Albright who believed in me, and my teammates—my brothers, who have given everything to get this far. We're going to win this. We have to win this.

I spot Iris standing in front of her seat, her parents to her side. Mr. Feldmore rarely attends the games, so it's good to see him. Iris waves, blowing me a kiss as she holds up a sign that says I love number ten and number eighteen, and it causes me to laugh. Beckett made her sign, but it's number ten in bold white letters that are on her navy jersey. Something about seeing my jersey on her chest almost does me in. With a final wave, I turn away and get in the zone. This game will take my complete focus.

Period one ends with a score of zero to zero. As Coach gives us his spiel between periods, I can't help but think how awful it felt on the ice. Nothing clicked. It's hard to explain, but some games run smoother than others. The games where everything falls into place and it feels effortless are the best kind—but this one isn't it. Our plays aren't working. Our passes aren't connecting. The freaking puck refuses to go in the goal. The Pittsburgh assholes and their trash talk won't let up.

The five starters—minus Dreven, who is already at the net—gather in a huddle in the center of the ice. "We got this!" Beckett yells.

We hit one another on the back, hyping each other up and get ready to start period two.

Period two feels as bad as one did though we did manage to score a goal, as did Pittsburgh. Stuck in a one-versus-one tie feels as shitty as the zero-point tie last period. Worse yet, I have this uneasy feeling in my gut, and I don't know why. I visualize scoring the goal and complete my breathing exercises and everything else that normally works to bring me to center and allow me to focus on the game. None of my typical techniques are working. My heart beats rapidly in my chest, but it's not from exertion. It's more anxiety than anything, and it doesn't make sense.

"Something doesn't feel right," I tell Beckett. "Maybe Coach should pull me."

"Are you kidding? No way. You're good. I need you, brother. It's a high-stakes game, is all. This is the closest we've been to the Cup in the past four years, and you're feeling it. It's normal. We can do this." He hits his gloves against mine. "We got this. Right?"

"Yeah." I exhale. "Let's get it done."

Pittsburgh's new defenseman, a twenty-two-year-old dipshit with anger issues for days, has been shit-talking for the whole game. As Coach instructed, we haven't taken the bait. Bash, Beck, and I should be given awards for the amount of restraint we've held this game.

I break away with the puck, moving toward Pittsburgh's goal. In a play we've been practicing, Bash skates toward the goal and eyes me as if I'm going to pass to him. Pittsburgh's left defenseman takes the bait and leaves Beckett to cover Bash. Without so much as eyeing Beckett, I slide the puck to him, and he stops it with his stick. Unguarded, he lifts his stick to make the shot that will win us the game when a flash of yellow and black flies into him. Beckett's body twists as the dipshit hits him into the boards.

A resounding thud and Beckett's pained cry sounds

as he falls to the ice. I see complete red when I catch a glimpse of the dipshit's cocky grin, and I charge. Fist raised, I hit him in the gut. Bash is at my side, punching the asshole in the arm. Helmets and gloves are thrown, and it's a mess of a fight.

Whistles blow, and the refs break it up. I fall to my knees at Beck's side. His eyes glisten with emotion as his face scrunches in pain. "It's bad," he chokes out, reaching for his knee. "I can't get up."

Rage fills me, and I want to pound the fucker's face into the ice. Instead, I'm led to the penalty box with Bash and Jaden. Less than five minutes are left in the period, which means the three of us will be in here for the remainder of the game.

The Pittsburgh asshole sits in the other penalty box as the medics come to assist Beckett.

My body shakes with anger as my best friend gets carried off the ice, not knowing the severity of his injury. Beckett has had many minor injuries over the years, but he's never needed a team of people to help him off the ice. My heart beats so loudly within, the whooshing of my blood is all I can hear. The surroundings fade as complete worry weighs on me. I barely flinch as Pittsburgh pulls a powerplay and rushes our goal with only Dreven, Max, and Beckett's sub left in the game. Even their goalie leaves their net for the play that scores them a goal. If I didn't hate them with everything I have, I could admit what an incredible move it was on their part.

The whole thing almost doesn't feel real. Beckett's hurt, and we just lost our chances for the Stanley Cup against a wild card team that shouldn't be here in the first place.

I drape my elbows on my knees and drop my head between my shoulders, completely defeated.

Inhale. Exhale.

This game felt all wrong from the onset, yet this is the worst-case scenario.

We've lost.

Heads low, we make our way to the locker room. We're out. We came so close just to lose it all like this in round one.

Sitting on the bench in front of my locker, I take in the empty spot beside me, usually occupied by Beckett. The adrenaline coursing through me abates, and the feeling of utter defeat and remorse hits me. Elbows on my knees, I rub my temples as angry tears fill my eyes.

I really thought this was the year we would take it all. I can't believe this is happening.

"Cade." Iris runs across the locker room, sits on the bench beside me, and wraps her arms around me, tears falling down her cheeks. "I'm so sorry."

"Beck?" I choke out.

"He's on his way to the hospital for an MRI now.

My parents are with him. I waited for you. We'll go together when you're ready."

I drop my chin. Standing from the bench, I head to the shower, anxious to get to Beckett.

As disgusted as we all are over our loss, the entire team occupies the waiting room at the hospital. We're a solemn group, that's for sure.

Finally, Hootie, the team's doctor, emerges with a beautiful woman at his side. He motions for us to come forward, and we do. The team circles around the pair.

"Gentlemen." Hootie's high-pitched voice grates on my nerves. "The MRI showed that Mr. Feldmore has a grade three MCL tear to his right knee. Thank you." He nods and takes a step back as if gearing up to exit.

"Wait!" I say, among similar protests from the rest of the team. "What does that mean? How long will he be out? What's the protocol to fix it?"

Tears to the knee ligaments are common in our profession, but the healing varies, depending on a slew of factors. I need to know what Beckett has in store for him.

Hootie holds up his hands to quiet us. "It just depends. There is no way of knowing."

The woman beside him steps forward. "A grade three tear usually takes four to eight weeks to heal. Mr. Feldmore got lucky in the fact that his ACL wasn't torn, as that would be a much longer recovery. He'll be in considerable pain for a few days and have tenderness and swelling in his knee. Right now, he needs to rest. Once the swelling goes down, he'll be fitted for a brace, which he'll wear to get around, and when he's ready, we'll start PT to get the knee in shape. If all goes well, he'll be ready to play before next season."

"Thank you," I say to the woman.

"Oh yes," Hootie adds, extending his hand to the lady beside him. "This is Dr. Elena Cortez. She's been hired as my replacement. I'm set to retire at the end of the season, and since you lost today, I guess that means I'm a retired man." The corners of his mouth tilt up at a weird angle, making him look more like a pelican than an owl.

The team murmurs to one another, confused at the sudden announcement. I'm sure not a single one of us is upset as Hootie is an awful doctor, but the manner in which we received this information seems odd. Then again, Dr. Hootie is nothing if not odd.

"Hello." Dr. Cortez moves her hand in front of her body in an awkward wave. "Yes, I'm taking over, effective immediately, so I'll be the one to monitor Mr. Feldmore's care, and I look forward to being a part of the Cranes organization."

Our new team doctor? I didn't see that coming, but I welcome it. Even if she graduated last in her class, she'll be heads above Hootie in skill. But I wouldn't be surprised if she graduated toward the top. It's obvious she's smart. Then again, next to Hootie, most people are geniuses. Another plus is she looks nothing like a bird of any sort. There's no other way to put it—Dr. Elena Cortez is stunning. She's on the taller side; I'd guess five feet eight inches. She's slender but curvy. She has big brown eyes and long brunette hair with golden highlights.

If Beckett has met her, I guarantee he's already inappropriately hit on her several times.

Iris comes into the waiting room and beckons me over. I leave the guys to question Dr. Cortez and follow Iris through the doors that lead to the patient rooms.

She takes my hand, and we make our way down the hallway. "Beck is asking for you."

"Thanks for getting me. The psycho at the front desk wouldn't let me through. Said family only."

Iris looks over her shoulder, her brow furrows. "Didn't you tell her you were family?"

"Well..." Her question catches me off guard.

She stops in front of a hospital room door. Releasing my hand, she grabs the handle. She gives me a soft smile. "You've been part of our family for sixteen years, Cade. You have to know that," she says before opening the door and motioning me in.

"Beck..." I groan when I see my best friend in the hospital bed. His leg, from his thigh to calf, is wrapped in a very cumbersome brace made of foam and plastic. "I'm so sorry, man."

He shoots me a classic Beckett Feldmore smile. "It's cool. Doctor says I'll be ready and in top shape well before the season starts."

"Yeah, well…" I huff out a breath. "It shouldn't have happened to you to begin with. The fucker from Pittsburgh. I swear, I want to beat his face in." Wanting to cause others physical harm isn't my normal vibe, but when an asshole hurts someone I love, I feel nothing but rage.

He shakes his head. "Believe me. I know. If I thought I could get away with it, I'd go burn his house down."

"Beckett!" Mrs. Feldmore gasps.

He rolls his eyes. "I'm totally kidding, Mom. It's an expression."

Mrs. Feldmore looks from me to Beckett, eyes big. "Not one I've ever heard."

"You know I'm kidding because I could totally get away with it," Beckett says.

I grin, happy he still has his sense of humor through it all.

"Well, let's just hope karma takes him out before next season," Iris states.

Mrs. Feldmore throws her hands up. "I did not raise you children to wish death onto others."

"Mom, chill," Iris says. "I don't want the guy to die. I'm just saying I hope something else happens in his life to cause him to leave the game before next season so the guys don't have to deal with him again."

"Yeah, what would do that other than a painful accident or injury? That's not kind, Iris." Mrs. Feldmore frowns.

Beckett scoots up in the bed, sitting straighter. "Like maybe his great-grandpa dies and leaves him a collection of ice cream trucks, and the douche decides he hates hockey, so he quits and discovers his passion has always been ice cream. Then he takes over his late great-grandfather's business and sells ice cream from a van all day." Beckett holds his mother's stare.

Iris points at Beckett. "Exactly like that, Mom. No pain inflicted."

Mrs. Feldmore rolls her eyes and turns to her husband, who sits in a chair in the corner of the room. "Can you believe them?"

"The guy took out your son's knee on purpose. Let them fantasize about burning his house down if they want."

"Yes." Beckett laughs. "And if I was caught, which as we've already gone over, I wouldn't be, Dad could totally get me off. Right?" He looks at Mr. Feldmore.

A rare smile crosses the man's face as he answers his son. "Absolutely."

Giving up, Mrs. Feldmore takes a seat in the chair next to her husband.

"What's up with this?" I motion toward the brace. "It looks like a six-year-old put it together."

"Yeah." Beckett scoffs. "It's all the hospital had. The hot doc ordered me a new one that will be delivered tomorrow. It's just to keep it immobilized while the swelling goes down. After that, I'll get a custom one that I'll wear to get around."

"I was wondering if you'd met her," I say with a sly grin.

"Hell yeah, I met her. She's better than Hootie by a thousandfold."

"That's for sure," I agree. "So are you staying here overnight?"

He shakes his head. "No. They should be getting my discharge paperwork around now, and I'll be good to go."

"You'll have to stop in the waiting room. Everyone is anxious to see you," I say.

"Will do." He nods.

Mrs. Feldmore pipes up from the corner. "We're taking him home with us so I can keep an eye on him." She sounds excited about the ordeal. She's always been an amazing mother. She probably misses having her kids under her roof. "You two are welcome to stay over, too."

"A Feldmore sleepover?" Raising a brow, I look from Beckett to Iris.

"Yeah, it will be fun." Iris's face lights up.

Mrs. Feldmore clasps her hands together, a wide smile on her face. "It will be just like old times."

I look at Iris with a smile. Not just like old times... so much better.

CHAPTER
THIRTY

IRIS

I t's been a month since the Cranes lost to Pittsburgh in game seven of round one of the playoffs, and for the most part, life has moved on. The guys still grumble over their performance and have pledged to redeem themselves next season.

Beckett has healed well and begun physical therapy. I have no doubt he'll once again be in top shape for the season opener in October.

As a girlfriend to an NHL player, I love the summer season. Cade still works out daily to stay in shape, but it's much more relaxed. After giving a hundred percent of themselves for seven months straight, the players need the summer months to recuperate. They continue to lift, work on skills, and condition, but it's more low-key and dependent on what each player wants to do.

Weirdly enough, there's a lot of golfing. Cade hits the greens several times a week with his teammates. I'm not much for golfing as a sport, but I can ride around in a golf cart with a drink in my hand like a champ.

More than anything, I'm happy—like truly, down to my bones happy. This feeling is surreal. After all these years, I'm finally who I'm supposed to be. And it isn't reliant on a fancy title or prestigious job. It's not the money I have in the bank or even who I'm dating. It's me living my life as my authentic self. Sure, Cade led me in the right direction, but I made the choice to be brave enough to live in the moment and stop pretending to be someone I'm not. It's been freeing.

I see the same kind of happiness in Cade, too, and I know he's experiencing a similar level of contentment as me. He's finally let go of the preconceived notions and insecurities that held him back. I guess you could say it's been a time of personal growth for us, and I'm so grateful we've been able to do it together. I've always loved Cade, but the depths in which I love him now are indescribable.

The other great thing about the summer months and the relaxed schedule is time off, which means vacations. I adore hanging out with Beckett and the rest of the guys, but I am over the moon excited to get Cade to myself for fourteen days.

I look out the window of my first class seat. Somewhere far beneath the visible clouds is the ocean as we fly to Hawaii. Cade rented us a house for the week right on the coast of Oahu.

The back of my head against the headrest, I rotate to my other side to take in the man sitting beside me. Earbuds in, he flips through the *Sky Mall* magazine. We were in almost the same position a mere six months ago, yet it feels like forever ago.

Feeling my stare, he pulls his AirPod from his ear and turns my way. "What is it?" He grins.

"Nothing." I shrug. "Just admiring you."

"Oh yeah?"

I nod. "And I can't wait to get there."

Reaching over, he takes my hand in his and squeezes. "Me too."

Hawaii with Cade has been a dream. In the week we've been here, we've been to a luau, a sunset dinner cruise, went parasailing, eaten at a delicious restaurant every night, frequented the shrimp and shaved iced stands along the beaches, shopped, and watched surfers at the North Shore. More than anything, we've snorkeled a lot. I'm looking forward to our adventures in the week to come. When we originally planned this trip, I thought two weeks away from home might be a lot, but it's not. In truth, I could stay here forever with Cade and be immensely happy.

The house we rented comes with private ocean access. Several yards beyond our sandy beach is a vast patch of coral with the most beautiful fish. Yesterday, we even saw a sea turtle.

I pull my fin onto my foot, and it snaps against my heel. Flippers in place, I secure the mask with the attached snorkel on my face.

"Ready?" Cade grins, looking ridiculous and adorable in his snorkel gear.

He extends his hand, and I take it. I pick my knees up high as we walk through the shallow waters, the rubber fins making it awkward to walk. Once we're deep enough to swim, I put the snorkel in my mouth while Cade does the same. We swim on the surface of the water, still hand in hand.

It's insanely romantic. I could do this every day and never tire of it. Everything beneath the surface of the ocean is so peaceful. The water covers my ears, drowning out the sounds of the world above. Groups of colorful fish swim by, ducking in and out of the paths in the coral. I take all the beautiful views in, my fingers entwined with Cade's.

Something moves to the right of the coral, and Cade points with his outside hand. I look to see a ray shake off some sand and slide along the ocean floor.

A large orangey-pink fish, almost the size of my head, swims straight toward me at face level. I tense up for a second, taken aback to have a big fish so close. The fish looks like it has puckered lips. Extending from its puckered lips are its gills that swoop back and upward, creating the allusion of contoured cheekbones. It's so cute, and right before it reaches my mask, it veers to the side with a flick of its tail fin. Cade squeezes my hand, and we continue exploring.

After an hour, we head back to our rental's sandy beach. When the water is shallow enough to stand, we do and continue walking toward the shoreline.

"That pink one with the kissy face was so cool," I exclaim.

Cade chuckles. "It was. Though it waited until the last second to change course, didn't it?"

"I know. Freaked me out a tad."

He reaches into the water and pulls out a grayish seashell. "It's an oyster. Maybe it'll have a pearl." The corner of his lips tilt up.

"That would be cool. But don't kill it if something is living in there."

"I won't. It feels empty, anyway," he says as we continue to shore.

I tug the rubber fins from my feet and pull the snorkel from my head.

With a contented sigh, I take a seat in the sand. Legs extended, arms out behind me, I look up at the palm trees shading me and smile. "I could live here. It's so beautiful."

"It is."

"We should rent a sailboat and do some sailing next week."

Cade tosses his snorkel gear at the bottom of the palm tree. His back is turned away as he situates his stuff, and he agrees. "Absolutely. That would be incredible." Standing, he turns and walks over to where I sit on the sand. He hands me the oyster shell he found in the water. "You should open it."

I hold the grayish-black shell in my palm, afraid to open it. "I don't want to hurt any creature that might be living inside."

"No living creature. I checked. But the interior is pretty cool."

Taking Cade's word for it, I flip open the top of the shell. My eyes go wide, and I gasp. Inside the shell is a stunning three-stone princess-cut diamond ring, the trio of diamonds set on a white gold band. The center diamond must be three carats, with each stone to its side a carat.

I blink several times, having difficulty processing what I see.

Finally, I look at Cade, who is on one knee. He reaches out and takes the ring from the shell and holds it out to me. "While we haven't been dating for a long time, I know there is no one else I want to spend my life with. You, my Rosie girl, have been my one love from the moment I knew what love was." He touches one of the smaller diamonds. "This diamond represents our past"—he moves his finger to the other smaller diamond—"and this one represents our present. But this one..." He touches the large center diamond and captures my stare, holding me in his gorgeous hazel gaze. "This one is our future. While our past and present are beautiful, our future is everything. You and I will have an amazing life together." He looks up at the palm trees overhead and smiles, returning his gaze toward me. "From here on out, the palm tree rule means something completely different. It means we share all the parts of ourselves. I want you to be able to tell me everything. I want to be the person you can trust with the most vulnerable parts of yourself, knowing that I will never hurt you. You are my everything. You are my one love. I loved you then. I love you now. And I will love you forever. Iris, will you marry me?"

Hot tears roll down my face. It's hard to describe what the moment you get everything you've ever wanted feels like, but it's pretty damn incredible.

"Yes," I choke out, nodding my head. "Yes. Yes. Yes!" I fling my arms around Cade, flinging myself toward him. We fall to the sand in ecstatic celebration.

I kiss Cade, my future husband, until my lips ache. We kneel in the sand, and I hold out my hand as he slides the stunning ring onto my finger. I hold my hand out, admiring the way the ring looks on my finger. "It's perfect."

"I'm glad you like it." He leans in and kisses me on the forehead.

"I can't tell you how happy I am." Emotion lodges in my throat.

"I know because I feel the same way."

Squinting, I look at him. "I can't believe you put this expensive ring in the ocean. What if it got carried away by the waves?"

He chuckles. "I only put the shell in the ocean. I had the ring hidden at the base of the palm tree."

"Oh, that makes sense." I stare at my hand.

An overwhelming sense of calm and contentment washes over me, and I'm filled with the greatest euphoria. I'm going to marry Cade Richards.

From here on out, my life will continue to be split into two parts: before and after.

Only now, it will be before this moment and after. The years spent before were dedicated to growth and self-discovery. Some days were incredible, while others were hard, but they all gave me something I needed—a lesson on which to develop into the woman I've become.

After this, though, well... it's everything. There will be hard times in our future, as is part of life, but the gift will be going through it all with Cade at my side. After this moment is the happily ever after.

After this moment is nothing but love.

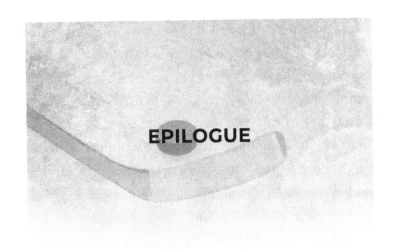

EPILOGUE

CADE

There's never been a bride as beautiful as Iris nor a man as lucky as me.

Putting together an extravagant wedding in three months would be a feat to most, but Iris, and the exceptional party planner she is, made it look easy. As soon as we returned from Hawaii, she got to work on the details. September in Michigan is the perfect time for a wedding. It's the very beginning of autumn and still warm and breezy. The trees are changing colors, which adds to the beauty. Best of all, it's preseason, so the entire team can celebrate with us without the time restraints we have during the season.

With our resources, we could've had any wedding we wanted and held it in the location of our choosing.

Exotic locations such as Fiji and New Zealand were on the table for a few hours, but ultimately, there was only one choice. We decided on her parents' home, and it's fitting. It's the place where we fell in love all those years ago. This isn't just any backyard wedding, however. It is stunning. Iris transformed the expansive yard into a whimsical garden with thousands of pink and white roses decorating the space, twinkle lights, and elegant decor. It's something straight out of a magazine, which is fitting since it will be in several.

"Just one more shot. Cade, can you kiss your beautiful bride?"

Beneath an arch of roses and green vines, I kiss my wife as flashes of light and clicks of cameras sound around us.

"Alright, ladies and gentlemen, the press portion of the wedding is over. Allow me to lead you out!" Beckett shouts, ushering the photographers from various magazines off the lawn.

"You're so beautiful," I say, running my hands down her sides. Her white satin dress clings to her body, caressing all her curves. It's simple but brilliant in design as it highlights the goddess that she is, making it near impossible for me to stop from ripping it off her and taking her against this floral archway.

"You better stop thinking what you're thinking." Her chest heaves in amusement. "I see your eyes getting darker, and we still have many hours before we can do what it is you're thinking about doing."

I run my hands over the skin of her shoulders and the narrow straps of her dress. "This dress is making it hard. It's like it possesses magical qualities of attraction," I kid.

"It's not the dress because I feel the same way about you in this tux. It's the fact that we're married, and that in itself is the best aphrodisiac there is."

"True."

She looks around me. "It looks like all the press camera people are gone. I still can't believe *People* magazine came." Iris shakes her head.

"Well, I am the Heartbreaker of the NHL and kind of a big deal," I tease before leaning in and kissing the tip of her nose.

She playfully slaps my chest. "Stop. Way too cocky. You sound like Beck."

"We have been best friends for sixteen years. He was bound to rub off on me sometime."

"Seventeen years," she says.

"You're right. I don't know how I forgot my twenty-seventh birthday." I laugh.

Beckett and I both have July birthdays, and a couple months ago, he threw a giant party to celebrate us, as he always does. Only this time, it ended with his engagement, which no one saw coming.

"I'll never forget that shocking night," Iris says, "and…" Her voice goes low as she pins me with a stare. "You are no longer the Heartbreaker. Remember?" She splays her hand across my chest and leans forward for a kiss.

I pepper kisses against her lips. "My mistake," I say between pecks. "Once again, you're right. I'm sure the cookies put an end to that name for good."

"They better." She laughs.

Iris had extra-large heart-shaped sugar cookies with pink frosting made up and wrapped to have placed at each place setting. The cookies read, "A heartbreaker no more."

The favors are adorable and delicious, but I'll wait to break the bad news to her. If one goes through so much trouble to tell the guys not to do something, you better believe they'll do it more.

"You want to dance?" I ask.

"With you? Always." Iris entwines her fingers through mine, and we walk over to the dance floor.

She drapes her arms over my shoulders, and I pull her close. As usual, we dance to a beat only we can hear, and it's mesmerizing. The amount of happiness I feel at this moment is unreal. Iris Richards is my wife. The wedding was beautiful and the decor stunning, but the only part that truly matters to me is the woman swaying in my arms. As long as she stood across from me and uttered the words "I do"—this day was bound to be perfect.

As I hold my wife amid the party around us, a level of contentment washes over me. The change happened so slowly, but for the first time, I realize that the critical voice in my head has completely vanished. None of the insecurities that took residence in my mind, making me feel as if I always had something to prove to be enough, are present. The departure was so gradual while building a life with Iris that I missed it.

I think of my mom and the words I said at her celebration of life. All of them still ring true, but now I recognize that it wasn't just her who saved me all those years ago. It was also the Feldmores. It was Iris.

Every meaningful word I used to describe Margaret could be applied to Iris, and I can't help feeling my mom here celebrating with me today. She's in my heart telling me I'm right where I'm supposed to be. Happy.

To echo the eulogy—my wife, my Rosie, my Iris is incredible and makes the world a better place. She changed my life for the better in so many ways. I grew into the man I am today because I love Iris. She made me feel as if I belonged. She loved me from the start when I couldn't even love myself.

I will love her for the rest of my life, and even then, when I take my last breath, I will love her still.

Dear Readers,

If you're reading this, thank you! Without you, I wouldn't be able to have my dream job. I hope you loved reading Cade and Iris's journey as much as I loved writing it. I know I'm late to the 'hockey romance' party. I've been wanting to write a hockey romance for a long time but I had to finish some other projects first. As I was writing One Pucking Love, I realized, more than anything, this is just an emotionally charged love story (like all my others), with a side of hockey lol. So hopefully whether you're a sports romance reader or a fan of my emotional reads, you loved this one.

I'm planning on Crane Hockey being a four-book series. But of course, if enough readers request, I can always write more. Next up is Beckett's book, One Pucking Heart! It will be released in five short weeks, and you'll love it!

I've said this many times, but this is a hard job. In truth, it's the most difficult job I've ever had, yet I love it so much. I love writing love stories with flawed characters who have to work for their HEA. Thank you for reading so I can continue to write.

Thank you for every social media post, share, or comment, every message, review, or recommendation to your book friends. It all matters, and it all gives

authors the fuel to keep going in a very brutal industry.
I truly can't express just how grateful I am to every
single one of you.

Make your life a beautiful one.

Forever,

Ellie 🩶

OTHER TITLES BY ELLIE WADE

For information on Ellie's books, please visit her website.

www.elliewade.com

The Choices Series

A Beautiful Kind of Love

A Forever Kind of Love

A Grateful Kind of Love

The Flawed Heart Series

Finding London

Keeping London

Loving London

Eternally London

Taming Georgia

The Beautiful Souls Collection

Bared Souls

Kindred Souls

Captivated Souls

Fated Souls

Destined Souls

Entwined Souls

The Crane Hockey Series

One Pucking Love

One Pucking Heart

One Pucking Wish

The Heroes of Fire Station Twelve

Fragment

Found

Fated

Standalones

Forever Baby

Chasing Memories

A Hundred Ways to Love

Cherry Blossom Grove

Ellie Wade's Sweet Collection

Licorice Wishes

Boxed Sets

The Flawed Heart Series

The Choices Series

The Beauty in the Journey Collection

Crane Hockey

ABOUT THE AUTHOR

Ellie Wade resides in southeast Michigan with her husband three children, and three dogs. She loves the beauty of her home state, especially the lakes and the gorgeous autumn weather. When she is not writing, you will find her reading, snuggled up with her kiddos, or spending time with family and friends. She loves traveling and exploring new places with her family.